Ground Rule
TROUBLE

Ground Rule TROUBLE

by
CHRISTMAS STAUDLE

THE LIBRARY OF CONGRESS HAS CATALOGED THIS EDITION AS FOLLOWS

Staudle, Chris.

Ground Rule Trouble/ Christmas Staudle.

Summary: A fun confidence building journey for all young teens. Sarah Trout, the star high school softball player must learn to balance family, friendship, and romance while cultivating her self-esteem on this roller coaster ride called high school. Mourning the recent death of her grandfather, a former major league baseball pitcher, Sarah attempts to honor him by pitching on the school baseball team.

    1)Sports-Fiction 2) Romance-Fiction 3) Friendship-Fiction

    LCCN 2020909857

ISBN: [978-0-578-70055-7]

Printed in the United States of America

https://ground-rule-trouble.com

ACKNOWLEDGEMENTS

This has been quite the enjoyable ride. First, I would like to thank my family. You have been there for me through all the ups and downs and this book never would have gotten done without all of you.

Thanks to Oregon Dave Jacobsen and Cressida Hanson for all their great editing; Michael Rosen for his valued input that's made this book better; Penny Weber for her outstanding cover illustration that reminded me every day this book was real; Steve Fishman for a lifetime of support and friendship; Mike Bellaria for believing in me from the beginning; The Redondo Beach public library for providing me a place to write and feel connected, and everyone else who has made a contribution to this book.

A special thanks to all the baseball and softball coaches from all over the world who share a common bond of ending every game and practice with the words "pick up your trash!"

Respect to Ricky Tan. Have fun. "A left will take you to the inter-state, but a right, will bring you right back here to me." Be Kind.

TABLE OF CONTENTS

Chapter 1
FAMILY

▪▪
▪▪

SARAH TROUT STRUGGLES to hold it together. Her sticky folding chair is missing most of its padding as it rocks back and forth on the uneven grass whenever she moves. This humid, eighty-five-degree weather is not typical for Redondo Beach, California.

Sarah's older brother Shane sits on her left, his chair seemingly more stable and *definitely* more padded than hers. She looks to her right and sees her kid brother, Andrew, and her mom, Kathrine. Her mom is wearing a black pantsuit and black Ray Bans, but also has a pink bow in her dark hair that matches a pink silk scarf.

An odd outfit for a funeral, Sarah thinks, but it is what Grandpa Al had wanted. A celebration.

Sarah takes a long breath to steady herself. The brisk on shore ocean breeze is blowing as the adjacent palm trees sway from side to side. The blue overhead canopy provides a pleasant shade covering for the carefully placed rows of mourners. She observes what seems to be a never-ending line of friends and family saying nice things about her grandfather, but she misses him too much to focus on their kindness. She feels guilty that she can't seem to celebrate his life with everyone else. It is all too new. She tries to cross her legs and catches herself as her chair almost tips over.

Grandpa Al had been a huge influence in Sarah's life. He'd prevailed for six months in his battle against pancreatic cancer. Sarah knew he had been in tremendous pain—knew his passing had been a relief to him—but the morning after she'd cried hard enough to cramp her stomach. It had been her job to take his old Kansas City Royals baseball uniform out of his closet so it could be placed inside his casket at the funeral. When she was alone in his room, Sarah recalled burying her face in the uniform to hide her sobs. The uniform had seemed to take forever to dry. Fortunately, she wasn't a mascara kind of kid.

I should be the one speaking up there, except I'd never make it through without bawling.

When Sarah found out about Grandpa Al's cancer, she tried to spend every spare second with him. If she wasn't at school, doing homework, surfing, or at softball practice — that stuff was non-negotiable — there was a good chance she was at Grandpa Al's bedside, pumping him for story after story . . . and some pitching tips as well. Many of her favorite stories were about how he got started in baseball.

Sarah reaches into her bag and pulls out the funeral program she was handed as they entered the ceremony. She begins to read through it:

> *Al Richardson grew up in Sayville, New York, in the early fifties. His dad was one of the last milkmen who worked the area from Bluepoint to Great River, six mornings a week—which meant Al's dad had the rest of the day to teach his son baseball. Al took to pitching like a Long Island duck to water. After high school and a brief stint in the army, Al signed a minor league contract with the Kansas City Royals for one thousand dollars. He couldn't believe somebody was going to pay him to play baseball.*

Sarah pauses for a moment, glancing up toward the bright blue sky. She reminisces to herself about Grandpa Al's excitement when he told her the story about signing his first baseball contract. She misses him terribly as she continues reading.

Al moved up through the Kansas City farm system with his fastball and slider. He was known for throwing inside, moving people off the plate. His dad, who had pitched on a Long Island barnstorming team, taught him how to throw the knuckleball, but Al had never pitched it as a pro. But as the competition became tougher, he needed to add a third pitch, and his manager told him to give it a try. Only a handful of pitchers can even throw the knuckleball, and even fewer batters can hit it reliably. Al with his new pitch, moved quickly from the minors to the majors, proceeding on to a very successful career with the Kansas City Royals as a knuckleball pitcher, retiring after nine seasons with a career record of 95–72.

Sarah stops reading and looks toward her mom who was watching her the entire time. She very neatly places the program back into her bag.

Kenny Ryder, a family friend for many years, is speaking at the funeral podium sharing stories of Grandpa Al from their younger days going out in Las Vegas. He gets a few laughs, with some anecdote about why casinos don't have clocks.

"When Al finished his baseball career, he didn't want to move back to the cold winters of New York. He always talked about the great weather playing baseball games in Southern California against the Angels. We spent a week driving around in his VW van, which I think he finally got rid of last year. We were always eating junk food, just looking for a place to live. As many of you know, that place ended up being Redondo Beach," said Kenny.

Kathrine politely smiles as he finishes. Her mind wanders, feeling the pain of her dad's passing taking its toll.

Sarah looks at Andrew. For a small kid he's got a big personality with a huge love of any kind of M&M Candies. For a five-year old boy, Andrew is definitely having trouble staying seated in his chair. He winds a strand of his curly blond hair around a finger and winks at Sarah while swinging his feet and kicking up some dirt.

Since their dad "checked out"— her mom's summary of him leaving, as if the family home had been a hotel—Sarah has played a major role in helping to raise Andrew. Kathrine is a good mom and works hard, but she teaches full time and manages the house. No one told Sarah to act like a second parent. It was just something she figured needed to happen. She still has sleepless nights wondering why dad just . . . left.

Her father's departure hurts Sarah's heart daily. She has been seeing a psychologist, an old friend of her mom, but the situation is a tough road for any fourteen-year-old.

Sarah feels her mom touch her shoulder as a loud truck door slams in the distance, breaking the somber mood momentarily. A handful of people turn their heads to observe cemetery workers unloading gardening equipment, which jolts Sarah back to the present.

Her mom looks at Andrew and mouths the words to Sarah, "Please take Andrew and let him walk around."

Sarah jumps at the chance to escape all the sadness and her uncomfortable chair.

"Andrew," she whispers, "let's go, buddy. We'll take a walk to see the ducks."

Andrew grins. He gives his mom's phone back, the soundless video game forgotten, and grabs Sarah's hand.

"Where are we going?" he says too loud.

"The pond." Sarah answers. "And shush!"

Andrew is not the world's best listener, but he is the world's biggest fan of his big sister. Sarah leads him down the aisle between the folding chairs and past a group of mourners standing in the back. When they're out of earshot of the funeral, she tells Andrew he can make noise again.

"Blah, blah, blah . . . what were all those people even saying?" Andrew holds up his hand and makes it talk like a puppet, as he skips down the path toward the pond. Surrounding large oak trees and thick green grass give the pond a serene feel as ten to fifteen various sized ducks float peacefully in front of them.

Sarah catches up. "Those people were talking about grandpa. They were saying what a kind and wonderful man he was."

Andrew stops. "They were?"

Sarah swallows. The best she can manage to reply is a nod.

When they reach the pond, Andrew chooses three rocks from the ground and draws a line in the dirt with the toe of his right shoe. He winds up like a pitcher and fires the first rock into the middle of the pond.

"Steee-*rike* one!" he hollers, acting as his own umpire.

"Andrew," Sarah chides, "you're gonna hit the ducks!"

He freezes mid-windup. "Ducks," exclaims Andrew. "Where?"

Half a laugh sneaks out of Sarah before she can stop it. Now she feels guilty again. But what if Grandpa Al would *want* her to laugh at his funeral? Was she letting him down by not laughing enough? She looks back at the crowd of people up the hill, gathered around the coffin of Grandpa Al. The whole thing stinks . . . dad leaving, Grandpa dying.... all of it.

"I know what you're doing Andrew," Sarah manages. "You're trying to make the ducks fly away."

Andrew smirks. "I *like* flying ducks."

"Dude, the ducks will fly when they're ready. We don't throw rocks at animals." Sarah continues sounding a bit more annoyed. "We actually don't throw at anyone—you know that."

Sarah smiles to herself, *unless they're crowding the plate.*

Andrew pauses, then tosses his final rock into the water. The ducks calmly paddle away from the splash and return to their floating lifestyle.

Sarah guesses this isn't the first time a young funeral-goer has tried to torment the ducks. She sighs and looks back toward the funeral service. A line of soldiers in dress uniforms lift rifles in unison toward the sky.

Crack! Crack! Crack! Three volleys echo across the cemetery. Tiny puffs of smoke float into the sunny sky. Andrew spins toward his sister, eyes wide. "Sarah?"

She explains as best she can about Grandpa Al's military honors—after which Andrew looks at her seriously and says, "I want a rifle."

Sarah can't help but laugh again. "Buddy, first let's focus on you actually brushing your teeth every night without having to be reminded, and *then* we can talk about getting you a rifle."

As quickly as it appears, the good feeling leaves. Sarah's back to sad, mad, confused, lonely—maybe sticking with just *sad* is easier. She finds a bench near the water's edge and sits. She pulls her knees up to her chest, wishing she were home in her sweatpants and flip-flops. She gazes at her brother as he watches the ducks, his hands flapping imitating them.

Sarah tries to distract him. "Hey Andrew. You still have that lightsaber from your birthday, right?"

It works. Andrew answers by leaping toward a nearby stick, grabbing it, and holding it in front of his face. *"Vroooom, vroooom,"* he says, striding toward the water's edge.

The ducks turn as a group and urgently float toward the far side of the pond.

Ducks forgotten and his stick swinging wildly, Andrew demonstrates his best Jedi poses.

Grandpa always loved Andrew's energy, Sarah tells herself. The happy sadness inside her is too much to handle. She pushes it away and tries to watch Andrew without thinking . . . anything. A few minutes later, Sarah turns to see her mother, a distant black-and-pink shape, waving.

"Come on buddy," she says, standing and stretching. "Time to go back. I think the funeral's over."

Andrew and Sarah walk slowly up the hill. Halfway to the gravesite Andrew stops. "Sis, will all these strange people finally go away now?"

Sarah drapes an arm around his shoulder and hopes it's comforting. "Don't get too excited kid. Most of the people here are all coming back to our house now."

* * *

The dented, full-length U-Haul merges onto Highway 99, heading south out of Fresno.

Stryker Estrada leans his head on the passenger window. Anyone on the road glancing his way sees a sharp jawline, olive skin, and a haircut that manages to look fresh and effortless at the same time.

His parents had dropped the news on him like a ton of bricks. They'd never talked about wanting to move or being unhappy in Fresno.

Stryker felt like someone kicked him—hard—in the stomach. *SoCal?* He even considered staying in Fresno and living with family friends until he finished high school, but once reality set in, living in Fresno for a few years without his family really didn't seem to make much sense.

Stryker had searched "Redondo Beach" on his phone and tapped *Images*—and what he saw wasn't exactly hard on the eyes.

The move makes total sense for his parents. Stryker looks across the cab at his dad, who is wrestling the oversized steering wheel and trying to keep up with the Ford F-250 in front of them, driven by Stryker's mom, with his six-year-old brother Jason constantly waving at them. His dad is getting a big pay raise *and* a system engineering position at SpaceX. The opportunity is just too good to pass up.

But for Stryker? It still wasn't easy. Moving to a new city had not been on his list of things to do during high school. Fresno is big enough, but it's still a farming town at heart, with real people living real lives. What he'd learned about Redondo Beach made it seem like people there only cared about the beach, Lululemon websites, and driving to hot yoga in Range Rovers.

Still, Stryker wasn't going to miss the constant dry heat of Fresno. There's no way to avoid it. But moving forward, the weather was the one thing he wasn't worried about.

New town. New school. New friends. New baseball team.

He shakes his head, and grins lopsidedly. That's a ton of new stuff—but maybe it is so new that it'll all work out somehow. He flips through a surfing magazine his uncle gave him as a silly going away present.

The beach should be great. I'm sure I can figure out how to surf, he thinks optimistically, *but how do I meet one of those cool surfer girls?*

Chapter 2

AFTER THE FUNERAL

■■
■■

THE DRIVE HOME takes forever, but Andrew manages to nap. Shane and Sarah spend the ride in silence while looking at their phones. Los Angeles freeways do not care about funerals or feelings. Traffic is not *sometimes* in LA—it is all the time.

Kathrine has invited most of the guests from the funeral back to her home to celebrate her dad's life. As she pulls the blue Honda CRV into the driveway, she sees her friend Lana's yellow convertible Mini Cooper is already parked. Lana, along with Kathrine's neighbor, Krista, volunteered to help set up for the wake.

Kathrine is glad she recently finished a round of upgrades to the backyard. Maybe her house isn't *quite* magazine-worthy, but she's proud of the new lawn, fire pit, furniture, and twinkling patio lights. She just wishes there were a happier reason to show off the upgrades.

"Shane, Sarah?" Kathrine calls over her shoulder. "Can you two please bring in the flower arrangements from the funeral? I bet you can find a good spot for them in the backyard."

"Yeah mom," says Sarah.

"Sure, whatever," mumbles Shane.

Kathrine turns her attention to Andrew. She taps the button to unlock the door on his side, then reaches back and rubs his leg.

"Hey buddy, we're home," she says.

Andrew opens his eyes while yawning, then stretches and groans.

"I know, afternoon naps are super groggy," Kathrine commiserates. "Head inside when you're ready. I've got to go help with the food."

Kathrine leaves Andrew's door open and enters the house. Instantly, she smells the tamales her friends are cooking in the oven. She knows that along with the tamales there will be a potluck feast in the backyard that reflects Redondo's diverse community: sushi rolls, pulled pork, homemade churros, lumpia. It looks like every United Nations country contributed a dish.

Kathrine walks slowly along the mantel, trailing a finger along the polished wood. She needs a moment to gather herself. Each photograph on the fireplace mantel adds to the timeline of her life: The latest school pictures for Shane, Sarah, and Andrew; Kathrine in costume with the cast of *West Side Story* from a community theater production she performed with. Then, the picture that hurts to look at, though she keeps it for the kids: her, the kids and Rick. Seventeen years together followed by five years apart....and counting.

Rick always struggled with alcohol. He had been sober for a time, but he eventually gave up trying. Kathrine made one last attempt to salvage their marriage with a weekend getaway to Palm Springs. On Saturday night they went out dancing, and after a few drinks, a few laughs, a few kisses, and a few good Prince songs, Andrew was created. Rick moved out—and moved on—the same day Kathrine told him she was pregnant.

The last picture conjures a grin, despite the day. Tucked in at the far end of the mantel is a team photo: Long Beach State Women's Soccer, 1997. There she is, crouched in the front row, scowling along with the rest of her team. That was the year Kathrine fractured the 5th metatarsal in her right foot and after a long rehab period, decided to focus on school full time, and stop playing soccer. She could still picture the look of pride on her Dad's face when she graduated at the top of her class with a teaching degree.

Dad loved me so much, Kathrine thinks. *He always did.* The only time she could remember him being prouder of her than on her graduation day was that day back in high school when Principal Rosen had suspended her from school. Her soccer team was having an intra-squad scrimmage with the boys' team, and Kathrine nutmegged a defender so savagely that he tripped and fell, drawing howls of laughter from his teammates. Moments later Kathrine was elbowed to the ground. She immediately jumped to her feet, chased the boy down, turned him around by the shoulder and punched him square in the face. The coaches would have wisely let things simmer down, but Principal Rosen happened to be strolling past on a tour of the school with some new board members. Feeling the need to make an example out of Kathrine, he ordered her to his office and announced she was being suspended.

When Grandpa Al arrived at school and heard the whole story from the very serious principal, he slapped the arm of his chair and exclaimed, "That's my girl!" Grinning from ear to ear, he took young Kathrine out to lunch and a movie. He probably told that story a hundred times over the years.

Kathrine takes a deep breath and wipes a tear from her cheek, then straightens the photo for no reason. It's time to join the party.

"Ladies," she announces, "it smells *amazing* in here."

Lana and Krista look up from their work. "Kathrine! How was the service?" asks Lana, giving Kathrine a hug.

Kathrine forces a grin. "About as well as can be expected at your dad's funeral. Father Paul was wonderful. And thank you," says Kathrine, looking around. "I don't know what I'd do without you two."

"Newsflash," jokes Krista, "your friends are here for you."

Kathrine groans and Lana chuckles.

Krista Stern is the 6 o'clock news anchor on Channel 5, and she cannot resist a good pun . . . or even a bad one. Normally put-together and proper, she places her hands on her hips and blows a strand of stray blonde hair away from her eyes. "Okay, even I know you can't make guacamole without avocados," she says looking around the kitchen, "but where did I put them?"

Mrs. Lana Berz, a close friend of Kathrine's who also teaches at the high school, points behind a bag of red Solo cups and says, "You mean these avocados?"

"Fresh set of eyes," laughs Krista, crossing the kitchen and grabbing the mesh bag.

"Careful, I already cut—" Half the avocados tumble onto the counter and roll onto the floor.

"Already cut the bag open?" laughs Krista again. "I just realized that."

Krista and Kathrine work together to pick up the avocados, while Lana removes foil trays of tamales from the oven.

"Mommy, mommy, mommy, mommy!" says Andrew.

The three women turn their attention to a still-sleepy Andrew who has wandered into the kitchen.

Now that he has their attention he announces, "I'm hungry."

Kathrine crouches down. "Andrew, I'm so proud of you. Today was hard. I'll get you food right now, okay buddy?" She moves to the refrigerator and asks, "Did you and Sarah have fun with the ducks?"

Andrew perks up. "Oh yeah—when we were with the ducks and heard the shooting, Sarah said she would get me my own *gun!*"

Lana and Krista both stifle a laugh or try to. They watch Kathrine to see how she navigates this one.

"I'm sure Sarah didn't say she was buying you a *gun*." Kathrine grabs a Tupperware of cut strawberries from the fridge and sets it on the counter. "At least not like those army men fired today. Here, hold this," Katherine says to her youngest son.

Andrew climbs onto a stool at the counter, then holds the container while Kathrine pulls off the lid.

"No, she—" begins Andrew. Kathrine pops a strawberry into his mouth, cutting him off.

"But I do know where we have a Super Soaker that cousin Brad got for you," she continues. "Remember how it was raining on Christmas morning? We never opened it."

Andrew grins and waggles his eyebrows.

"So, finish your strawberries, wash up, and change into some play clothes. Shane can take you out front and you guys can shoot it out there."

"Why not the *back* yard?" asks Andrew.

"We have guests and food back there," explains Kathrine. She sees a sly smirk cross Andrew's face. The Super Soaker idea might not have been her best, but she's moving full speed ahead on her promise now.

"Gonna throw some more ice and drinks in the cooler here, Mom," says Shane.

Kathrine looks up and sees the first few guests filing into the backyard through the side gate.

"Thank you, Shane," she says.

"Mom?" Sarah asks, "what can I do to help?"

"Honey, we've got things under control here. Why don't you go out back and welcome our guests?"

"Sure," Sarah agrees, turning toward the door.

"And Sarah?" Kathrine calls as her daughter turns. "How are you holding up?"

Sarah lets the door close and reenters the kitchen. "I was doing okay for a while, but driving home I realized that grandpa is . . . actually gone," admits Sarah.

Kathrine crosses to Sarah and pulls her into a tight hug. "Grandpa was ready to go, Sarah. He loved you so much, and he was so proud of you."

Sarah finds some relief in the kind words. "Thanks, Mom. I love you," she whispers, wiping tears from her eyes. "I'm going to head out back and grab some food."

While Sarah and Kathrine are talking, Shane drops the stocked cooler by the back door and cuts across the kitchen, heading for his room instead of the backyard.

"Shane!" Kathrine calls out.

He stops but doesn't turn.

Kathrine lowers her voice. "Shane," she says, "you're not going to be hibernating in your room while we have all this company. I know it has been a hard day, but I need you to go find Andrew and play with him."

Shane sighs, "I know. Andrew's told me ten times already."

Kathrine takes care of the final details in the kitchen, as Sarah walks to the table of potluck food outside and is pleased to see someone has brought her favorite: macaroni and cheese.

"Sarah!" calls Mrs. Berz.

Sarah looks up from the food to see her mom's friend and science teacher. They embrace.

"How is softball going?" Mrs. Berz asks. "Your mom says the team should be good this year."

"Season's just getting started, but it's going well, thanks," Sarah replies. "It's been so windy though."

Mrs. Berz laughs. "Windy?"

"Yeah, like super windy."

"You know how my nieces play college softball?"

Sarah nods.

"Well, the youngest, Alexa, plays at Colorado Mesa. They practice outside. In February. In *Colorado*! Those conditions will toughen you up."

Sarah politely smiles, thankful she plays near the Pacific Ocean and not the Rockies. Sarah glances toward the backyard gate and sees her close friend Kayla, and a few of the girls from her softball team arriving, along with Coach Dan from baseball.

Dan Sugimoto heads up the baseball program at South Redondo Beach High School. The girls greet Sarah as they beeline for the carne asada.

"Softball girls got to eat!" Annemarie playfully shouts as the girls grab paper plates and load them up.

Coach Dan finds Sarah first thing. He makes eye contact with her. "Are you doing okay, Sarah? I know your mom is worried about you."

Dan is a police officer by trade. Besides coaching the high school baseball team, he is also Andrew's T-ball coach and has known the Trout family for many years. Dan recruited Sarah to help out with the coaching of Andrews team, which she enjoys. Sarah and Coach Dan have had more than their fair share of baseball discussions over the years, and she can tell he truly loves the game. She can also tell that Coach Dan and her mom are getting to be good friends. She's just not sure, how good . . . or how she feels about her mom possibly dating. Sarah has fished for more information a few times, slyly asking her mom what she thinks about Dan and teasing her about him being cute, and pretty buff. Her mom would either laugh off the idea or reply that she does not need her daughter to play matchmaker even if he is cute and buff.

"It's been hard," Sarah replies to Coach Dan. "But I'm hanging in there."

"You know, your grandfather and I had some long talks about baseball," chuckles Dan. "Mostly about how the game keeps changing!"

Sarah agrees. "That sounds like him for sure!"

"He was a first-class gentleman," says Coach Dan fondly. "The real deal."

Sarah waits. She loves hearing the stories.

"Well, when *his* grandfather passed away, a few months later his dad—your great grandfather—gave Al a letter. When he opened it, he discovered it was from his grandfather—your great-*great*-grandfather—and it talked about how proud he was of Al for playing baseball, and keeping the baseball tradition going in the family. The letter explained his love for Al and how his whole family supported what he was doing. Kind of reminds me of your family right now, Sarah. A love for baseball, softball, but more than that, a love for each other."

Sarah breathes deeply and nods. "Thanks for sharing that. I've never heard that story." She is still thinking about the letter when Dan breaks the silence.

"So . . ." Dan says.

Sarah knows that usually means a new topic.

"Speaking of baseball and your grandfather, he and I used to also talk about how well you can throw a knuckleball. That's really very impressive. Not many *adults* can throw that pitch, let alone hit it. Have you ever considered playing baseball and pitching on our high school team?"

Sarah would be lying if she says she hasn't. Somewhere deep down, she likes the idea of pitching in a baseball game and striking out boys.

"Yeah, at times," Sarah admits, "But how would it even work? I mean, I've already got school and surfing and softball."

Dan nods, letting her process.

"And my knuckleball is decent, but I've never pitched against a batter in a real game." She's not afraid of the competition—not that afraid anyway—but dealing with the boys on the team is low on her list of priorities. Sarah has spent enough time around Shane and his friends to know how boys are when they get together. There are obviously good guys, but a group of high school boys together almost always means somebody is acting like a fool and being immature. The last thing she wants is to stand out as some kind of target for their antics, or worse. Still, she *would* be doing it to honor Grandpa Al.

"At least think about it," Coach Dan suggests. "We've got an open baseball tryout next week, and I'd love to see you out there."

The lower the sun sinks the more the Trout's backyard swells with laughter. Bellies are full, empty bottles and cans cram the recycling bins, and enough stories of Grandpa Al have been shared to write a book. Kathrine is pleased. This honors her father the best way possible: Happiness.

Kathrine, chatting with Lana at one of the food tables, is startled by the feeling of cold water dripping from her hair and running down her neck. To a chorus of laughter, Kathrine turns around to see Andrew leaning out of Shane's second story bedroom window, blasting his Super Soaker at the crowd of guests below.

"Andrew *James!*" she yells, "stop getting people wet! And please get out of that window, you're going to fall!"

"I can't fall out! Shane is holding my legs," crows Andrew. He continues to spray the backyard as guests scramble to get out of range. The encouraging laughter is clearly more important to him than his mother being upset.

"That's *not* the answer I was looking for!" scolds Kathrine as she hustles inside.

Two of Shane's surfing buddies, Harry and Will, dodging the water, reach one of the food tables and begin chucking uneaten Hawaiian rolls at Andrew. They score a few direct hits, but most of the rolls just bounce off the house. The attack causes Andrew to briefly stop firing, but as soon as the last roll is tossed, he renews his assault.

The rest of the high schoolers in the backyard begin to rhythmically chant. "Andrew! Andrew! Andrew!"

CeCe, one of Sarah's softball friends, is videoing the whole scene. "I'm gonna post this for sure!" she hollers.

Andrew yells back, "I've got my own online videos too!"

A fresh round of laughter erupts from those watching.

Three weeks earlier Andrew spent hours with Sarah, recording himself sliding on the wooden floors in the hallway as he practiced stealing second base. Andrew made it clear he was stealing second base and not third base. Sarah posted the best video for him, after which Andrew would not stop bragging about the twelve likes he got.

Kathrine stomps upstairs. *Wouldn't that be the perfect end to a perfect day. A funeral and then a trip to the ER.* She pushes open Shane's door, not bothering to knock. Andrew is no longer hanging out the window, but he is unscrewing the lid on the water gun's tank. Andrew is startled by his mom's quick arrival and fails to notice the water pouring out of the tank and onto Shane's desk, backpack, and carpet. Kathrine mentally reaches down and *draws* one more bucket of patience from the well, probably her last. She knows it has been a hard day for the kids too. She knows they are coping as best they can.

"Shane, please grab some towels from the hall closet and dry off your stuff," the calmness in her voice surprises her in a good way. "I don't want to get things ruined."

He nods and steps into the hall.

Before Kathrine can think of what to tell her little troublemaker, Andrew follows his brother into the hall and darts the opposite way toward the stairs.

Shane returns to his room with a couple of old beach towels and hollers after his brother. "Andrew, get back here! You helped make this mess so help me clean it up!"

Too late.

Kathrine takes one of the towels and mops the top of the desk, then the backpack. "Thank you for watching him," she says. "It got a little messy, but you guys seemed to be having fun."

"Fun?" Shane is pushing a towel into the wet carpet. "That's not exactly the word I'd use."

Kathrine smiles at her son. "Well, at least you didn't drop your brother out the window . . . and at least he didn't pour water on your laptop."

Done soaking up the water, Kathrine and Shane drape the towels over the back of the door and look together out the window into the backyard. Andrew races around the lawn, high-fiving the remaining guests, asking if anyone else brought a water gun. Kathrine steals a glance at her seventeen-year old junior and sees a look cross his face. It's the good kind of older brother look, the one that means despite everything, he still loves his little brother, and maybe even likes him some of the time.

Kathrine moves closer to Shane and puts her arm around his shoulders. "How are you doing, honey? I know it's been a tough week."

Shane doesn't answer. He stands up tall and stares into the yard. But then something changes and he slumps a little, leaning his head into his mom's shoulder. "I know I shouldn't say it, but the funeral sucked," he admits.

Kathrine bites her lip. *Let's him continue.*

Shane takes a shuddering breath and scrubs a thumb across each cheek. "The whole thing made me sad. The speeches, the ceremony, people saying sorry for your loss, all of it. I realize that I'm really the man of the house now. When dad left us, we still had Grandpa. But now it's just me."

Kathrine's heart feels like it will explode with all the love for her oldest son. She risks a small joke. "Unless you think maybe we should let *Andrew* be the man of the house?"

A half-sob, half-laugh bursts out of Shane.

Kathrine hugs him tightly. "I love you, Grandpa loved you, and there's still *plenty* of time for you to be a teenager Shane. We're a family, and we'll figure things out as a family, we'll figure things out together."

Shane nods into her shoulder, then separates. He takes a couple of deep breaths to compose himself. "Some of the guys are still here. I'm going to head down to the backyard."

"Okay, honey." She gives him a playful tap on his butt as he leaves, then lets herself sink into Shane's bed.

Shane was not wrong about the man-of-the-house thing, despite what she told him about staying a teenager. She would fight for his right to be a kid, but life had a way of changing things without asking for a second opinion.

Kathrine's dad moved into the house five years earlier, making a home for himself in the guest room. He was a father figure to all three kids, filling the role Rick had abandoned. He talked Shane through bad first dates and helped him discover his passion for surfing. He played countless games of catch and pickle in the backyard with Sarah, even teaching her to carry on the family knuckleball tradition. And he chased Andrew around as best he could, delighting in the constant jokes and laughter, even as his body began to fail him. Grandpa Al had been a constant presence in their lives. Sarah is right: he's *actually* gone. The Trout's are back to four again, and Kathrine isn't sure how she's going to cope.

"I know you were ready to go, dad," she whispers. "I know you were. But *I definitely* wasn't."

* * *

The breeze flowing through the newly rented house in Redondo Beach was a welcome relief from the dry hot Fresno summers, they had left behind. Stryker and his family have finished unloading their life's possessions from their rental truck and are taking a little break before they begin to put things away.

"I see a bunch of dead bugs in the kitchen cabinets and some of the bathrooms; that can't be a good thing," says Stryker as he sits on a pile of boxes assessing what needs to be done next. "And that refrigerator is making a ton of weird noises. It sounds like a bad marching band."

"I'm having the whole place cleaned tomorrow, so don't get caught up in what the place looks like now," says Stryker's mom, as she sits on the couch going through her folder with all the new school enrollment information. "Tomorrow, I'm going to sign your brother up for elementary school, and then I'm going to the high school for you. Coach Breen emailed me from Fresno that he spoke with the high school baseball coach here and talked you up. The South Redondo coach said he is happy to have any good new players who work hard."

Stryker, feeling a bit uncomfortable with so many unknowns moving forward, walks over to the large bay window and stares off at the ocean in the distance.

"I know we just got here, and the area seems great, but going to a new school, in the middle of the school year, dealing with making friends, not something I'm looking forward to."

His mom walks over to him and gives him a big hug. "You've been successful in the past, there is no reason to think that's not going to occur here. Just be yourself, things just take time."

"I know. It's just being the new kid, not knowing anyone, it doesn't sound very fun," complains Stryker.

"Well, I've been going through the school packet. There's a spring dance Enchantment Under the something ocean," as she flips through the folder. "Here it is, Enchantment Under the Sea dance. Sounds fun. They do it every year. You've worked on school dances in Fresno. This could be an easy way to volunteer and meet some new friends once things settle down."

"I guess, but working all those dances with Madison," Stryker pauses. "Actually I really don't want to talk about this, and get all that started again, but I will think about it," says Stryker.

Stryker's dad comes in from closing up the truck. "Just saw four girls riding bikes in their bathing suits carrying surfboards heading down to the beach. We are definitely not in Fresno anymore."

Stryker and his dad high five each other while laughing as his mom shakes her head.

"Glad you boys are having so much fun. Let's see you high five each other after carrying that dresser and those mattresses upstairs."

"You're no fun," replies a smiling Stryker.

Chapter 3

NEW SEASON

⬛

T HE SOFTBALL FIELDS at South Redondo Beach High School are not lush and green by accident. The grounds crew takes pride in the condition of the grass, and despite the mild climate they have their work cut out for them every spring. In fall, the combination of multiple soccer teams practicing tears up the grass, but come opening day of the softball season, the fields always look immaculate.

South Redondo Beach High has a history of winning softball championships, and the support from the community is always strong. Sarah hopes this year her team will add another banner to the fence surrounding the field. They'll have to take it one game at a time, as the saying goes, but today is a good place to start. It's a Saturday, their first softball game of the year, and Westwood High should not pose too much of a challenge.

The all dirt netted bullpen is already full of shells from discarded sunflower seeds as Sarah tries to warm up. Even from the bullpen she can sense the excitement in the air. There are easily one-hundred-plus softball players from younger city leagues enjoying the festivities. The high school boosters have set up a bouncy house, tables with baked goods, face painting stations, and even a booth to see how fast you can throw a softball.

The mood is fun and light. Most of the players parents arrived early to stake out good seats for themselves and the grandparents.

Sarah looks but can't see her mom. Kathrine is probably chasing Andrew around somewhere. Sarah laughs to herself as she sees Kayla frantically waving hello in the distance wearing her beach volleyball jersey with yoga pants, and a blue bandana around her neck, as she walks barefoot toward the bleachers. Kayla is Sarah's best friend. They've been in most of the same classes since kindergarten. Kayla has long black hair, and a sense of style. The girls try to support each other when they can, even with their busy schedules.

Sarah throws a few more warm-up pitches to her catcher, Annemarie, and tries not to think about what the boosters are serving at the snack bar. In her opinion, the other sports boosters put together decent enough snack bars—except basketball, which is terrible—but softball is in another league. Fans can find breakfast burritos, shredded beef, double cheeseburgers, chicken and rice....

Focus, she tells herself. *Start the season right.*

Coach Nevs calls the girls in from their final warm up. While the other girls clear the infield, Sarah and Annemarie jog in from the bullpen in right field. She was only a few strikes short of her warm-up goal, so she should be ready to go.

"Let's bring it in girls," Coach Nevs says, clapping his hands as they arrive. "Come on, bring it in, bring it in." Once the girls are paying attention, he continues his pregame pep talk. "We've got a nice crowd here today, probably the biggest we've had for a home opener in years. So, let's show 'em what we can do. And listen, whoever hits the first home run today, I'll buy you a hot fudge sundae at Farrells."

Katt chimes in from the far end of the dugout. "Coach, Farrells's *closed* like two months ago!"

Coach Nevs breaks into a big smile. "It *did?* Well then, it looks like I'll be saving a few bucks," he laughs, beginning to do the floss dance. "Still got it! Still got it! People love me! Still got it!!!

Most of the girls roll their eyes or sigh. CeCe sticks her finger toward her mouth in a gag-me motion. A few others can't help giggling.

Coach Nevs focuses on the positive, looking at the laughers. "You girls get me," he says. "You realize how funny I am."

"If you mean watching you *trying* to dance," laughs Annemarie, "you're hysterical."

Sarah loves this. It's part of what makes her team and softball so fun. Coach Nevs has coached the softball team for ten seasons. Sarah remembers learning his name when she was still in elementary school. Grandpa Al would bring her to games whenever he could, hoping to inspire her. More than once he told Sarah, "Coach Nevs is a good guy, but he knows nothing about coaching." Sarah quickly learned with a grandfather who played pro baseball that he is pretty much critical of all coaches. Sarah likes Coach Nevs energy, and how patient he is when he's coaching, but more importantly she respects how he treats all the girls.

Sarah looks around the dugout. She has been on the diamond with a bunch of these girls since she was in first grade. Over the years they have practiced together, driven to club tournaments all over California together, been scolded for breaking quiet hours at hotels together, and eaten way too much junk food together.

Katt plays shortstop and pitches, despite barely topping five feet. Growing up her coaches never really gave her a chance to pitch, but Coach Nevs couldn't care less about how tall a pitcher is *supposed* to be. Katt has one of the strongest arms on the team, which earned her the nickname "toy cannon."

Annemarie, the catcher, is a big-time batter. She always leads the team in home runs. At times she can seem a little lazy, but when it really counts, she will step up and nail a clutch hit. The girls all know to check Annemarie's bat bag when searching for snacks.

Mia plays first base. Sarah met Mia at a dance class at age six and they have been friends ever since. Mia is also the fastest girl on the team—*and* she's faster than a bunch of the boys on the baseball team.

CeCe plays second base and is the team wild card. Some days she's focused and plays great, and other days Coach has to yell at her to put her phone away *during* a game. CeCe comes from a large Samoan family and can be an intimidating figure, on and off the field. Her dad is a Marine Sargent and does his best at keeping her focused.

"Ladies, ladies," Coach Nevs says, bringing Sarah back to the moment. "I know some of you would like to watch me dance all day . . ." He waits patiently for the boos and groans to die down, still smiling enthusiastically, ". . . but we've got a ballgame to play!"

Sarah winds up, throws, and . . . it's *another* ball. The batter tosses her bat toward her dugout and trots down the line toward first base, whipping up the Westwood fans with her raised arms. What was supposed to be a winnable warm-up game has turned into a nail-biter. South Redondo Beach is up 4-3 in the top of the final inning, but there's only one out and Sarah has been having trouble throwing strikes all game long. Now the tying run is on first, and Sarah's not sure she's got "the stuff" to get the job done.

"Two more outs," Sarah mutters as the next Westwood batter steps to the plate. "Two lousy little outs. Come on, Trout!" When she falls behind in the count 2-0 to the next Westwood batter, Coach Nevs asks the umpire for time and jogs out to the mound.

Sarah looks at the ground, but that doesn't prevent her from hearing the Westwood fan who is yelling at the top of his lungs.

"Walk this batter, too—we *love* walks!"

That's all the encouragement the Westwood fans need. A chant begins. "*More* walks, *more* walks, *more* walks . . ."

Coach Nevs arrives at the mound. "How you feeling?" he asks, hand in front of his mouth in the secretive tradition of all managers. He continues without waiting for an answer. "This game is still yours if you bear down and throw strikes."

Sarah would argue that the umpire needs stronger glasses. In Sarah's opinion he's had trouble seeing correctly for most of the game. But Coach Nevs is right. They can still win. She can finish this out. She is wearing down, but she's still got the fire. This is her game.

Sarah squares up to Coach Nevs, "I'm fine. I got this," she says.

He looks at her for a few seconds. "Let's put them away," he says. He nods and jogs back to the dugout.

This is not the first close game Sarah has handled before. She's optimistic the game will end well. Coach Nevs has watched Sarah pitch both games of a double header in club softball tournaments in 100-degree heat and gut out close wins.

As Sarah waits for the batter to settle into the batter's box, she thinks to herself, *how did I get into this mess?* She's feeling a little more confident after Coach Nevs' pep talk. She uses her right foot to adjust the dirt on the mound and takes her place on the rubber. She checks the sign from Annemarie. Fastball, inside.

Sarah nods, winds up—and delivers her pitch . . . directly toward the Westwood batter. With no time to jump away from the pitch, all the batter can do is turn her back and flinch toward the umpire before the ball arrives.

Smack—right on the numbers! The batter and the ball both drop to the ground. The ball rolls a few inches across the dirt and stops, but the batter writhes in pain.

The boos and yells erupt from the Westwood fans and players. "That was intentional!"

"Throw her out!"

"C'mon, ump!"

The coaches from Westwood hustle out to the injured batter and help her to her feet. She rubs her back gingerly, and trots slowly down to first base.

Grandpa Al has taught Sarah to never be afraid to pitch inside, but this was a ball that definitely got away from her. She felt a little bad that she'd hit the opposing player with her "that will leave a mark" fastball, but Sarah won't be losing any sleep over it. Trouble is, this is still a one-run game, and Sarah's just put the *go-ahead* run on first. That, combined with a hit batter has riled up the fans on both sides. There's a real tension in the air as the crowd grows louder and more boisterous than it has been all game.

In their dugout the Westwood players rhythmically chant, hoping to get their runners in. "Ducks on the Pond—ooh-*ah!* Ducks on the Pond—ooh-*ah!* What's going on? Ducks on the pond—yeah!"

The South Redondo Beach bench is yelling encouragement to Sarah, "You got this Sarah, you got this!"

The home fans are chanting full force. They do not want this one to get away from them.

"*Let's* go, Re-*don*-do!"

The opposing fans smell blood in the water. They sense they might steal a win from the mighty South Redondo. "West-wood! West-wood!!"

Sarah composes herself on the mound. Or tries to. Doubt is creeping into her mind about her fastball. The next batter steps into the batter's box. Sarah takes a deep breath and checks the ball in her glove. She plans to keep it simple: throw it hard and low. Even if the Westwood batter makes contact, chances are the ball will stay on the ground.

Sarah shakes off two signs from Annemarie until they're on the same page. She's just about to begin her wind up when she catches a movement in the corner of her eye. Something like a large dog has darted onto the field and is kicking up dirt.

As Sarah turns to look, the home plate umpire turns his volume all the way up. "Time *out!*"

Sarah, her head completely turned now, can't believe what she sees. *What the*—It's her kid brother in his dirty baseball uniform, sprinting full speed, churning his little legs so fast they're a blur. Fans from both sides shift their attention and quickly begin to hoot and laugh.

Andrew, running flat-out, crosses the third base line and heads toward second base. Katt, playing shortstop, steps up with a big grin on her face, planning to grab Andrew as he runs by. But Andrew, using his best football fake, cuts around Katt's outstretched arms and continues running.

Sarah suddenly understands what he is going to do. She shakes her head at her crazy little brother. And sure enough, Andrew, still at full speed, completes a perfect feet-first slide into second base, kicking up an enormous cloud of dust as he hits the bag. Apparently, all that practice sliding on the wood floors at home has paid off.

The crowd—Westwood fans, Redondo fans, girls in both dugouts—erupts in cheers.

Andrew pops up from his slide, turns to face the stands and grins. The applause and hollers swell. Everyone loves what's happening. Everyone except Kathrine, who is already out of the stands and headed toward third base.

Andrew runs back the way he came, intersecting with his mom near the third base fence.

"Andrew!" Kathrine scolds, crouching down to grab his shoulders and look him in the eyes. "You could have been hit with a bat or a ball or run over by a player! And there's a *game* going on!"

Andrew knows that what he did was wrong, but he can't help asking, "Mom, did you see me slide?"

"Yes, Andrew," she huffs, "everyone saw your slide. But I don't ever want to see you running onto the field during your sister's game again. Actually, you can't run on the field during *anyone's* game!"

Andrew understands that he's in trouble with his mom. There will be consequences and he will take the heat. But he can't help feeling better when he returns to the stands and some of the dads start high-fiving him for his daring display of base running.

"Looking good out there, Andrew!" says Annemarie's dad. "If the girls ran the bases like you, we might have a few more runs today!"

Everyone around them enjoys the laugh as Andrew's smile grows wider.

Another dad leans over and shows Andrew the video on his phone. "Check it out . . . you can add this to your collection!"

Even Kathrine is smiling now. Andrew appears to have turned his bad behavior into mini-celebrity status.

But everyone's attention instantly snaps back to the field when the home plate umpire yells, "Play ball!" The umpire puts his mask back on. There's still a game to play.

The crowd on both sides of the bleachers had focused on Andrew's antics, but now the tension floods back. The score is still 4-3 South Redondo Beach, with one out in the top of the last inning.

Watching her brother slide into second was just the break Sarah needed to calm down and settle in. She winds up. Strike one! Sarah's starting to feel confident. She checks the sign, settles in again, winds up, and fires. This time the Westwood batter tracks Sarah's fastball and cracks a line drive down the first base line. The Westwood fans rise in anticipation of a double into right field, a hit that might even score two runs. But this was not to be Westwood's day—not with Mia playing first base. She takes two powerful steps to her right, leaps into the air, and at full extension snags the ball in her glove. Then, catlike, she scrambles back to first base and tags it with her glove, just ahead of the sliding Westwood base runner who had been halfway to second. Double play, three outs, inning over, game over—and just that quickly South Redondo Beach wins 4-3.

The Redondo fans erupt with cheers as Sarah and the rest of the team sprint toward Mia to celebrate. After many high fives and hugs, the girls walk the base line toward home plate and shake hands with the Westwood players. A ritual as old as the game itself: *Good game, good game, good game, good game, good game, good game, good game, good game, punk, good game, good game, good game, good game, good game. . .*

However, Westwood's coach, Mick Martin, is pissed and looking a bit disheveled with dirt all over his outfit as if he played in the game. He's right in Coach Nevs' face, practically shouting.

"I could swear your pitcher was throwing at my girls, coach." He waits a second for a bigger audience and gets one as the girls and some parents quiet down to listen. "*Intentionally!*" He says the last part like it's a curse word.

Coach Nevs has coached against Coach Martin for many years. They've even coached some All-Star teams together. Coach Martin currently has a foster child, Joey Smoak, who even plays baseball on the South Redondo Beach High School team. This kind of behavior is not surprising from him, but the accusation just isn't logical.

"It's a *one run* game," responds Coach Nevs, annoyed, "so it would make no sense to hit one of your batters on purpose. What would be the point? As he pauses, "Do you think I had that little kid run on the field just to play with your mind?"

"I just want to let you know," steams Coach Martin, "that I'm filing a complaint with the league. In fact, I'm calling the league commissioner as soon as we're done here!"

"Listen, Mick, do whatever you need to. That's why the commissioner makes the big bucks, eh?"

As Coach Martin storms off, the South Redondo Beach girls collect all their belongings and exit the dugout area, filtering their way into the crowd. Parents swarm the girls.

"Great job, Sarah," Kathrine says as she finds her daughter. "Proud of you and all the girls. Things looked a little shaky out there for a while!"

"I had trouble getting the ball over," admits Sarah. "And that ump didn't seem to help much."

"Spoken like a true pitcher," Kathrine chuckles. "I'm just glad you girls won."

A couple of the baseball players, Dylan and Evan, stop by to congratulate Sarah.

Annemarie, standing near the group, turns to CeCe and whispers, "That Evan is a cutie."

CeCe puts her hands on her hips in a playful sexy pose "new couple alert, new couple alert."

Annemarie, a bit embarrassed, elbows CeCe playfully in her side to be quiet.

As the boys leave, a group of young softball girls in their uniforms approach Sarah. Their parents stand in a group behind them, taking pictures. The smallest girl Kelli is bouncing up and down. She turns to her mom who tells her, "Well? Go on!"

"When we got out of the car, I told everyone I could see it was you from our softball camp. I'd know you anywhere, and you're my favorite player, Sarah. I knew it was you."

"Awww," Sarah coos. She can't remember hearing a longer or a sweeter sentence in her life. "Of course, I remember all you little monsters," she banters. "Now get over here and gimme a hug!"

As the parents take even more pictures, Kelli the young softball player asks Sarah, "Does that boy always run on the field and slide? That was funny!"

"No!" laughs Sarah. "That was the first and hopefully the last time. That was my little brother, Andrew, and he may be in a bit of trouble."

Andrew, standing nearby next to Kathrine, hides behind her legs as the young girls' giggle at him.

Only a few yards away, Westwood's Coach Martin is having an animated phone conversation, presumably with someone from the league office. "This has happened way too many times! Yes, I know it's only the first game, What? What do you mean *how* many? I just told you—*way* too many! She's *gotta* be suspended! She—"

Just then one of the youth softball teams walks past. Every single girl is wearing cleats and dragging a heavy bat bag. The wheels on their bags, combined with their cleats, make a shockingly loud racket on the concrete.

Coach Martin shouts something inaudible into his phone and then pulls it away from his ear. He stares at the youth team, making a "hurry up" motion with his free hand. As the final girl walks past, the noise quiets down. Coach Martin raises the phone back to his ear. "Sorry—so annoying! Anyway, I was trying to tell you that—"

At the same moment, one of the youth team's coaches looks at her phone and announces to the girls, "Wait, girls—field change, we're now on lower field *one*, not field 2! Let's go, turn around, come on, come on! We've gotta go warm up!"

Like a procession of military soldiers marching in a parade, the girls turn around in unison and walk back the same way they came, dragging their bags in loud harmony directly past Coach Martin for a second time. Once again, he is forced to pull the phone from his ear. He gives the girls an angry glare to get them to move faster . . . until the second-to-last girl stops. Grins.

"Hi Coach Martin!" she says. "You coached my sister, Remy!"

Coach Martin is taken out of his foul mood for a brief second and gives a friendly wave to the young girl as she continues past. Looking slightly less insane now, he returns the phone to his ear. "So sorry about all that! Anyway, now that things have settled down, I was saying that I think Sarah Trout should be—hello? Hello?! Oh, for crying out loud!" He pockets his phone and wanders away, muttering to no one in particular, "They hung up on me . . . this really isn't my day!"

* * *

The South Redondo Beach High campus transforms each night. Gone is the daily hustle and bustle of teacher and student activity. The parking lot empties, except for a few remaining cars belonging to custodians and campus security. The darkness creates a safe haven for those who do not belong. A weathered coyote makes his way across the turf football field, searching his regular garbage cans for dinner. The track meet earlier in the day has given him plenty of leftover options.

Inside the school, an entrance door is eased shut near the athletic training room. Joey Smoak, a South Redondo student and baseball player, sneaks down the small dark hallway, using the flashlight on his phone to guide him. Joey scouted the hallway earlier and knows there are no cameras—a level of effort and preparation he would never apply to his schoolwork.

Joey has come up through the foster system. He never really felt like he fit in anywhere, and his erratic temper hasn't helped his case. Getting shuffled from family to family to family is not exactly a recipe for stability. His current foster parents do the best they can. Joey doesn't hate them. It's just that he has decided he doesn't need any family now. He is better off on his own. His older brother's been living on his own since he was a teenager, and Joey wants to do the same. . . minus his older brother's jail time.

Joey continues down the hallway, staying close to the wall. His goal is the school's administrative offices. Once inside he rifles through drawers, searching for money or anything he can sell online or at a pawn shop. An envelope marked "pizza money" contains forty-eight dollars that he happily stuffs into his pocket. He considers grabbing a laptop. His brother has shown him how to disconnect the trackers—but before he decides, the sound of a door closing in the distance startles him. The cash will have to do tonight. Joey retraces his route as quickly and quietly as he came.

Once outside, running toward the football field, Joey looks back. The zigzagging lights through a set of windows tell him that two guys from campus security are patrolling. Good thing he bailed when he did. When he reaches the far side of the football field, Joey leaps partway up the fence, wedging his right foot into a gap in the chain-link. He starts climbing, until a movement catches his eye and causes him to freeze. Hanging from the fence, he turns to the left and looks: just local wildlife. A coyote trots across the field with a characteristic white-and-red paper bag in its mouth. *In-n-Out Burger*, Joey thinks. *Looks like it was a pretty successful night for everyone.* A moment later he disappears down a dark street into the night.

Chapter 4
NEW FRIEND

SARAH HUSTLES OUT of the car, backpack over one shoulder, and she jogs toward the main entrance at South Redondo Beach High School as her mom drives off to the teachers parking lot. Depending on the day, and Shane's surfing schedule, this is how Sarah gets to school. Starting the day by hustling is standard procedure for Sarah. One of her superpowers is hearing every alert her phone makes *except* her alarm. This leads to frequent discussions with her mom on weekday mornings about responsibility, timeliness, and the possible locations of her homework, backpack, sweatshirt, and so on.

Sarah dodges a small group of students talking as she enters the building. Freshman year hasn't exactly been easy for her. She spends time worrying about how to fit in, whether people will like her, how to balance homework, sports, and friends, all while trying to process Grandpa Al's passing which isn't making it any easier.

Knowing some of Shane's buddies has definitely helped. Sarah hears more than the average number of "hellos" in the hallways, thanks to being his kid sister. On the other hand, her brother's buddies are not exactly the best "bats in the dugout"—most of them are more like T-ball bats if she's being honest. Dealing with their immaturity is usually more trouble than it's worth.

Still, between Kayla and her softball girls, Sarah thinks she has a pretty good number of friends. But making more never hurts. That is one of the reasons she and Kayla signed up to be on the spring dance committee, which is the reason she's now jogging. School hasn't started yet, so she's technically early, but she still might be late for the planning meeting. She can hear Mrs. Berz' voice in her head— *"Enchantment Under the Sea* isn't going to plan itself!"—and picks up her pace.

Sarah quickly stops by the softball locker room to drop off some clean practice pants and socks. The recent funky smell and crunchy socks were a strong indicator it was time to do laundry. Sitting on the hallway floor outside the gymnasium are Dylan and some other baseball guys waiting for Coach Dan.

As Sarah approaches them from a distance, Joey Smoak mumbles to Dylan, "She's cute."

Dylan responds, "No boyfriend."

Joey playfully forces some ice cubes from his drink down Evans shirt as Dylan urges him on.

Evan scrambles to his feet to get away from Joey and the ice, and crosses paths with Sarah. "Hey Sarah, need any ice?" Evan says as he struggles to reach the ice cubes from underneath the back of his shirt.

"I'm good," says Sarah as the ice from Evan's shirt spills onto her and the wet floor.

Joey laughs loudly as he pulls the remaining ice cubes from his cup and throws them at an embarrassed Evan.

"You guys are a mess. Stay away from me," says Sarah annoyed, as she walks over to Dylan and gives him a hug hello.

Dylan Berouty lived two streets over from the Trout's until seventh grade, before his family moved to a new house in Palos Verdes—a nice big house. When Dylan was living in their neighborhood, he spent a lot of time in the backyard with Shane and Sarah. Dylan's mom, Bridgett, is a big-time corporate lawyer who is reaping the rewards of all the hard work she has put in since her days at Stanford Law. Dylan is a great kid who usually has a good head on his shoulders and has remained friends with Sarah.

"What are you up to girl? Hope these guys didn't mess up your stuff," Dylan says as he releases Sarah from their friendly embrace.

"Got my clothes wet enough to annoy me," as she frowns and wipes the water off her shirt while glaring over at Joey and Evan who are still fooling around.

Joey walks over toward Sarah. "Hey, sorry about all the water. My intention wasn't to get you wet," says Joey sounding genuinely apologetic to Sarah.

"Thank you, it really wasn't that bad," replies Sarah smiling.

"We're just waiting for coach. He's got some new stuff-- uniforms, bats, and some sweet new warm-ups for us to check out," says Dylan.

Sarah, who has had discussions with Coach Nevs about the softball team needing new equipment is disappointed with Dylan's news. "I can't believe baseball is getting more new stuff. Our softball gear is so old. Coach Nevs said there was no money for us. That stuff should be ours," says Sarah.

"Baseball should always get the best. People love baseball. I'm sure softball can have our old uniforms when we're done with them," jokes Dylan.

"That's not how the world works these days Dylan," replies Sarah.

Joey not realizing Dylan is joking around, cuts in, "Come on dude! Have you been living under a rock? Everyone knows girls' sports are equal to boys. And the last few years softball has won some league titles."

Sarah knows of Joey from the baseball team, but has never spoken to him until now and is pleasantly surprised by his point of view. "Thanks Joey, but I'm sure Dylan is just kidding," replies Sarah as she glares at Dylan.

Dylan confidently places his hands on both of their shoulders while smiling. "I'm just playing, you know that Sarah, I love softball."

Sarah gives a wave goodbye to the boys as she heads off to her dance meeting.

Joey quickly follows her as Evan and Dylan look on. "Hey, wait up, it was chill talking with you. I know we hardly know each other, but maybe we should go out some time, go see a movie?"

Sarah, having very little experience being asked out by guys, is surprised by Joey's boldness. She barely knows him, and he was acting like a fool getting her wet when she arrived. "Sorry, I'm not really looking for that right now, but thank you," replies Sarah as she continues down the hallway to her meeting.

Dylan and Evan, who could hear their conversation, both crack up laughing.

"Wooooooooo!!! She shut you down," says Dylan.

"Ouch!!! What a burn!" says Evan.

Joey turns bright red, the veins in his arms start to bulge, as he looks on in anger, humiliated, by Evan and Dylan's comments. "Screw you guys!! I should kick both of your asses!" Joey fumes off, kicking open the exit door hard with his foot, and heads outside.

"Yo Joey, relax! We're just joking. What's your problem?" shouts Dylan after him.

The dance committee meets in the science wing of the school. Sarah reaches the last corner of the hallway when she sees Coach Dan walking toward her with a boy she's never seen. She stops and stares. Coach Dan looks like Coach Dan: friendly, kind, and yes, surprisingly buff. But the boy *with* Coach Dan looks . . . well, there's no other way to say it. Super cute. Like somebody she'd like to know.

Coach Dan makes a beeline toward her, along with the mystery boy. Sarah's pulse starts to race. She tries to look casual but is not sure it's working.

"Hey, Sarah!" says Coach Dan warmly. "Lemme introduce you to Stryker. He recently moved from Northern California and he's playing ball with the school team now."

Stryker smiles at Sarah.

God he's cute, she thinks. After a slightly-too-long pause, she reaches out her hand. "Hi, Striper" she manages, "nice to meet you." Her hand was warm in his.

"*Stryker*," Coach Dan corrects, chuckling, "it's Stryker, not Striper."

"*Stryker*," Sarah corrects herself. "Sorry, nice to meet you."

His smile widens as he releases her hand. "No problem Sarah, my name can be a little confusing to people. I've been called lots of different names my whole life," replies Stryker politely.

"Sarah," interrupts Coach Dan, "I'm grabbing Stryker some baseball gear now, but if you get a chance later, can you stop by my office? I need to speak with you for a quick minute."

"Sure," she answers. "I probably can this afternoon." She assumes Coach Dan wants to talk more about her trying out and pitching for the baseball team. Sarah turns and watches as Coach Dan and Stryker head toward the locker room.

I'm such a fool, she thinks. *He's so cute and I didn't even get his name right. Stryker! Stryker! Stryker! This must be that new kid Katt said something about, from Fresno. That's northern California, I think.*

Frustrated with herself, Sarah continues down the hall. She can't help but smile when she reaches the door to Mrs. Berz's classroom. Plastered on the front of it is one of those "Hang in There" cat posters, except someone with a Sharpie and considerable skill has transformed the adorable kitten into a terrifying monster. She pushes open the door and finds Kayla waiting with the rest of the dance committee.

Glancing at her phone, Sarah realizes she is actually two minutes early. A minor miracle. She goes straight to the chair beside Kayla and sits, then immediately leans closer and confesses, "I just met the cutest boy, but I acted like such an idiot!"

Kayla pays immediate attention. "Tell me *more!*" she whispers. "Who is he?"

"His name is Stryker, except I—"

"Stryker?" interrupts Kayla. "That's a cool name!"

"I know," agrees Sarah. "I called him Striper by mistake. He just started here recently. He's tall, dark hair, great smile, maybe Latino."

Kayla makes the "go on . . ." motion with her hand.

"And he's *legit* hot. And on the baseball team."

Kayla laughs. "Great, just what you need—*another* cute baseball player!"

Sarah refuses to take the bait. "This one seems different . . ." She trails off, frowning, then tries to finish. "He's just . . . I don't know, *different.*"

"Yeah, well wasn't that guy visiting from San Diego last summer—Dustin, right? —wasn't *he* supposed to be different?"

"Yeah, yeah," admits Sarah. "After being around Dustin for a few days I couldn't get far enough away from him. He was always *trying* to rap Jay Z songs and was always flipping his hair every minute. Dude was a mess. I don't think Stryker is like that."

Kayla raises her eyebrows. "Well, I'll keep my eye out for this Stryker dude."

Sarah is quiet for a moment, then whispers to Kayla, "Also, his hand was so strong, but it still felt soft and warm."

"*What!?*" Kayla exclaims too loudly. Both girls look around the room in embarrassment.

Kayla switches back to a whisper. "Whoa, whoa, whoa, stop the clock—you're telling me you held his *hand?* You just met!"

"I shook his hand when Coach Dan introduced us," answers Sarah.

"Since when do you shake hands with a guy you *just* met? You normally give the 'what's up' head nod," she says, demonstrating with an upward nod that Sarah returns, "but you went *right* for the hand? This could be serious!"

Sarah and Kayla can't help giggling, which turns into laughing—but before it gets out of hand, Mrs. Berz bustles into the room pushing a cart with overstuffed bags and boxes overflowing with dance supplies.

"Good morning, people. Thank you all for being here on time. I wish I could say the same for me!" Lana Berz is the head of the science department. During school hours she teaches Geology and Physics, but right now she is the driving force behind the spring dance.

Sarah has known Mrs. Berz forever, from her friendship with her mom, and loves her to death. This isn't the first "Enchantment Under the Sea" dance, and it won't be the last. Sarah's been coming to the dance for years, thanks to her mom and Shane. She remembers the first time she watched the classic movie, *Back to the Future*.

"Hey, Marty McFly is at the same dance that *our* school has, Mom!" Sarah had exclaimed. "Enchantment Under the Sea!"

Her mom had explained that South Redondo Beach High School copied the idea from the movie, thanks to Lana Berz' obsession. When Lana was a young girl, her dad, who was a Marine serving overseas, took her to see *Back to the Future* on one of his rare visits home. Lana had never forgotten the experience, and now her classroom features a section devoted to memorabilia: an original movie poster with the words "Science is your Future" taped neatly in the upper corner, a scale model of a DeLorean (complete with a flux capacitor), and a signed headshot of Michael J. Fox. Mrs. Berz had once admitted that she had seen the movie more than one-hundred times. But that isn't the only reason for the dance name. "Enchantment Under the Sea" is also a fundraiser for "Motion in the Ocean," a local nonprofit that works to keep beaches clean and safe. That's a big deal in a place like Redondo Beach, where everyone is directly connected to the ocean. If you don't surf, swim, fish, ride a bike, or go for walks, you at least appreciate the gorgeous views and weather.

The fundraiser is another reason Sarah has volunteered to help with the dance. Protecting her beaches is high on her priority list. A few years back, Mrs. Berz also incorporated a local high school baseball tournament as part of the weekend festivities. Between the dance and the baseball tournament, it has brought a lot of publicity to Redondo Beach, along with much-needed funding to help protect the environment.

Letting go of the cart, Mrs. Berz picks up her notebook full of committee logs. "Let's get to it," she calls out.

The waiting student committee members turn their full attention to her as she waves the notebook in the air for all to see.

"We have two weeks, people. *Two weeks.*" She taps the notebook with her free hand for emphasis. "I know we have lots of new members, but your committees should be *way* past the idea stage, and you should have an operational plan in place. By the end of the day I need you to send me your plan in writing so I can go over it, got it?"

She receives a round of good-natured groans in response.

"And remember kids, this is a community event that many people take pride in. It's our responsibility to help make it great. Tickets sales and sponsor donations generate *thousands* of dollars to help our charity, and this year will be no different. Now I'll let you get to work."

Sarah whispers to Kayla, "We need to find some more people to help with the setup. Mia and CeCe said they were maybes, and Shane said he'll try to get a few buddies to help."

"You sure Shane and his buddies will want to set up for a high school dance?" Kayla asks.

"Surfer dudes care about the ocean," Sarah answers. "Besides, my mother will make him if he refuses!"

"Well, I'll add his name along with CeCe and Mia when I send our plan to Mrs. Berz later," says Kayla as she flips through pictures of previous Enchantment dances. They did some great stuff with dolphin and octopus' cutouts, plus frosty blue waves, but . . ."

"But what?" asks Sarah. "Don't tell me they also—"

"Don't worry, don't worry," interrupts Kayla proudly. "I didn't find a single picture of what *we're* going to do! I'm so excited to see it!"

"We've still got a ton of work," agrees Sarah, "but I'm excited too!"

As the girls sketch out ideas and jot down notes, a loud knock on the closed-door startles them.

Mrs. Berz shouts a friendly, "Come in!"

The door swings open and Sarah jumps a little. *It's Stryker.* He looks uncomfortable as every eye in the room fixes on him.

"Are you here to work on the dance?" Mrs. Berz asks kindly. "And you are?"

"Stryker!" Sarah is shocked by the sound of her own voice. She could have let Stryker speak for himself. She could have let Mrs. Berz handle things. But no, she had to blurt out his name, loudly. She feels her cheeks heating up. Now everyone in the room is looking at her.

"Stryker," she repeats, hoping she sounds chill enough. "He's new, and his name is Stryker."

Mrs. Berz doesn't miss a beat. She's already halfway across the classroom and holding out her hand. "Well then, Stryker, nice to meet you. I'm Mrs. Berz. And you're here to help with the dance?"

"Thanks. Nice to meet you." Stryker shakes her hand and smiles. "I was on the dance committee at my old school, so I thought maybe . . ."

Mrs. Berz clearly lives for moments like this. "Well, you've come to the right place. We can always use help the last few weeks leading up to the dance."

"Great," he says, nodding. "So, should I . . .?"

Mrs. Berz does a quick survey of the room and checks her clipboard. "Let's see—we're pretty well-staffed. Hmm . . .

why don't you sit in with the decorations committee. No matter what we'll need help setting up and cleaning up." She points toward Sarah and Kayla as she says this.

Sarah lets out a tiny gasp. Not because of Stryker, but because Kayla has just kicked her beneath the table. Sarah manages to turn her gasp into a smile, and then she pivots to what she hopes is a laid-back head-nod.

"And you already know Sarah," Mrs. Berz continues. "So, it'll be perfect!"

Stryker strolls over to the table where Kayla and Sarah are sitting.

Kayla takes charge. "Hey, I'm Kayla. What's up?" She and Stryker nod to each other. "And this is Sarah, but I guess you already knew that. Have a seat."

Sarah is so grateful to Kayla. Thanks to Kayla doing a super-normal introduction, chances are near one-hundred-percent Stryker doesn't realize Sarah and Kayla have been talking about him.

"Nice to meet you Kayla," Stryker says. "What's up, Sarah."

"Hey," Sarah responds. Still recovering from her earlier blunder.

"To be honest, I'm not sure how much I can help out." Stryker grabs a chair and spins it backwards before sitting down. "I just wanted to see how things work here, you know?"

Sarah starts to relax a little. "That's fine. Kayla and I pretty much have the big things covered. Just stop by whenever you can. There's always something to do." Sarah assumes Stryker's going to leave now, and maybe she'll see him at the next meeting, and she'll be ready by then, except he keeps talking.

"With baseball practice, homework, and helping my folks with the move . . . life's pretty busy right now. But I have some time to help out now. What would you like me to do?"

Kayla and Sarah pause and look at each other.

"Well, if you can help a bit now, why don't you and Sarah go through the checklist to see what decorating supplies we need," says Kayla as she's tapping Sarah's foot under the table. "Most of the stuff should be in those boxes on the cart, but if we're missing something, just make a list and we can go to the store."

Stryker walks over to the cart, grabs a big box, and carries it to a free table. He dumps out the contents of the box, sits, and starts spreading out the items.

The girls are far enough from Stryker that Kayla has the chance to say, quick and quiet, "This is like that old movie, *High School Musical*, like when Zak Efron meets Vanessa Hudgens. It's almost magical, right? The guy you like just walked in the door and joined our committee!" "Right?"

Sarah is still in shock. "But what do I say?"

"Just go over there and get your head in the game girl," Kayla chuckles. "Make some small talk. He looks a little lost. Go, go, go."

Sarah *mostly* trusts her best friend on this. So next thing she knows, she's sitting at Stryker's table. "I can read off the items we need," she suggests, "and you can tell me if we have them."

"Got it," Stryker responds confidently.

"Let's see . . . three plastic clams for entrance display?"

"Lobsters, dolphins, sharks, what I think is a freaky sea-horse," he says, sorting through all the items, "and some starfish—wait, actually they may just be regular stars . . . but no clams. Oh-for-one, not the start we're looking for."

"Wait," says Sarah, as she quickly runs through her list of supplies. "I don't think all the stuff has been brought up from the storage unit yet. I'm definitely missing a box. I bet that's where the clams are."

Mrs. Berz surveys the room like a captain on a pirate ship. She's listening in on all the group conversations at once. Years of experience does make a difference. "Sarah you are correct. Mr. Berz still has a bunch of stuff in his car trunk from the weekend.

He's supposed to bring it by later today. You should move on to something else besides the checklist."

Sarah and Stryker face each other across the table. He's looking down at his phone. Sarah takes the chance to glance at him without being noticed. She isn't sure what it is about him.

He seems kind of confident yet shy at the same time. Definitely looks good in those jeans. He's taller than me. We would look so good as a couple in selfies. I really hope he doesn't have a girlfriend.

When he looks up, his question catches her off guard. "What's next, Sarah?"

"What's next? Let's see . . ." *Why can't I think of anything? Why is he just staring at me?* "We can just . . . um . . ." Sarah's a nervous wreck now. She can't seem to get any words out, and for some reason her hands feel wet. He's just looking at her calmly, waiting for an answer.

Fortunately, he interjects. "I was sorry to hear about your grandfather passing away." Stryker pauses for a second and continues, "After we met in the hallway, Coach Dan told me about your grandfather's funeral, and about how he played baseball in the majors, and what a great man he was," says Stryker.

Sarah sits up straighter. Relieved he spoke up first. "Yes, thank you. It's been a rough few weeks, if I seem a little out of it. But thank you."

"That's okay, I'm sure you've been through a lot," Stryker says. "Losing a loved one can be really emotional." He reaches across the table and gives a comforting touch to her arm.

Sarah smiles at him.

"Like Jeter, our cat! When he died last year, I was a disaster for *weeks*," says Stryker. It takes about a millisecond for Stryker to realize his comparison. "Crap, I am *so* sorry! I *definitely* didn't mean to compare your grandfather to my cat!"

Sarah's been going through a lot, sure, but she's still watching him. Processing. And the sweet smile on his face shows that he did not mean to be rude. He was just trying to help.

"I didn't take it in a bad way at all," Sarah assures him. She's smiling now. "And I'm sorry to hear about Jeter too. I bet he was a Hall of Fame cat, first ballot."

Stryker laughs right away.

Sarah can think again. She's feeling a lot more normal now. "So, you were asking what's next? We should probably start..."

Briiinnnggg! Briiinnnggg!

"The bell, I should probably get to class," Stryker finishes, picking up his phone.

"Let's exchange contact info in case we need to get a hold of you," says Sarah.

As soon as they exchange info, Stryker heads for the door.

"Thanks for helping out!" Sarah calls after him.

"No worries," replies Stryker over his shoulder, and just like that he's gone.

Kayla appears at Sarah's side quickly. She grins and says, "Well, *that* was entertaining!"

"I know, I know," Sarah admits. "I made a fool of myself. I was so nervous around him."

"You sounded fine," soothes Kayla. "I should know because I was listening to your whole conversation. Seriously, though, getting all his info was very smooth. You were *fine*, promise."

Sarah sighs. "I don't feel fine," sounding emotionally exhausted.

"Instead," jokes Kayla, "do you *feel* fine about World History class? Because that's where we've got to be in, like, three minutes."

Chapter 5

THAT WAS FUN

███

SHANE IS BEHIND the wheel of his silver Jeep Cherokee, windows down with Ariana Grande blaring, as he cruises up to the front of South Redondo Beach High School to pick up Sarah after school. A lot of guys would hide their love for Ariana Grande, but Shane is a big fan and can handle the teasing. Not to mention he enjoys the extra attention he gets from girls when they find out. Shane knows how to work it.

Shane and Kathrine made a deal: he could choose the car he wanted within reason, instead of some ugly clunker, as long as he helped out with shuttling Sarah and Andrew around when needed. Shane doesn't mind the deal at all, and now he's waiting patiently like an Uber driver to take Sarah to her volunteer job helping with Andrew's T-ball team.

Kathrine believes it is important for her children to be involved in the community. Ever since Shane was in junior high school; the kids have been involved with a civic group called HELP (Healing Earth Learning Program) that connects volunteers with projects around the city, such as storm clean up and clothing donation. When Coach Dan asked Sarah if she was interested in helping, she said yes right away. Sarah thought it would be a great way to get volunteer hours and hang out with her little brother.

The minute Shane observes Sarah exiting the school, he pushes down hard on his horn and holds it long. He begins laughing out loud when he sees the mortified expression on Sarah's face as she walks by a group of staring students. Sarah finally reaches the Jeep and yanks open the back door.

"What is your problem? First Ariana, and now that stupid horn!"

Shane still laughing says, "If only you could have seen your face. You looked so pissed off! C'mon, that was funny!"

Sarah tosses her backpack and sweatshirt into the back seat and jumps in. "You're so embarrassing," she says as Shane wheels his Jeep onto Beryl Ave.

Shane's a bit confused. "Wait, why are you even in the back? I'm not your chauffeur!"

"I'm changing into practice clothes. I don't want to get my good clothes dirty."

"Good clothes? You call shorts and a Hobie T-shirt your good clothes?"

"Very funny," she answers sarcastically.

Sarah pulls out sweatpants and an old T-shirt. She nonchalantly begins pulling off her shorts in the car—she's had years of practice, changing in the car between school and various team practices.

Shane gets an idea. Since they're still right in front of the school, he starts blowing his car horn again, over and over trying to draw attention to Sarah changing. He yells out the window to no one in particular, "Woohoo! Crazy girl in the back! Woohoo!"

"What is wrong with you?!" exclaims Sarah.

Just then, Shane checks his rearview mirror to see a police car with his lights on pulling up closely behind him.

"Pull over!" commands the voice on the police loudspeaker.

"Dammit," Shane says, turning off the stereo. "Are you kidding me?!"

Sarah simply reaches down, grabs a beach towel from the floor of Shane's Jeep, and finishes changing. She is finding some amusement in their situation: her brother is the one in trouble, but she is a little nervous for him.

"Have fun explaining to the cop why you're blowing your horn so much and yelling like an idiot," says Sarah annoyed. She's now fully dressed, and anxious to see how her brother handles this.

Shane is stressing. He fumbles for his driver's license while attempting to pull over safely. "You better be quiet back there! Crap, I'm not sure where my registration is. This can't be good."

The Jeep Cherokee settles to a stop on the west side of the street. The police officer pulls up behind the Jeep and immediately exits his vehicle. The officer confidently strides to the driver's side door cautiously looking into the car. Shane sees him approaching in his side view mirror and lowers his window down all the way.

"Is everything okay?" the officer asks. He's wearing mirrored aviators and his uniform is impeccable. "I heard you blowing your horn over and over. I couldn't tell if you're just goofing around or if you really need help."

"I'm sorry officer, we were just fooling around." Shane's head and shoulders slump as he hands the officer his driver's license, even though the officer never asks for it.

The officer looks at the license, takes off his sunglasses, and focuses on the passenger in the back. He breaks into a big smile.

So does Sarah.

"Well hello there, Sarah. Everything okay?"

"Coach Dan! Until you took off your sunglasses, I didn't recognize you in your uniform! You look so important." She's pretty sure Coach Dan won't write Shane a ticket.

Shane is a little confused how the officer knows Sarah until he realizes it's Coach Dan. He shakes his head and ventures a smile.

"I was just heading to practice when I heard all of this horn blowing and thought someone might need help," said Coach Dan.

"Just my dumb brother thinking he's funny, blowing the horn trying to embarrass me while I'm changing for practice . . . if that even makes any sense."

"I have sisters too, so I guess that *is* a little funny," chuckles Dan. Shane breaks into a wide grin.

Dan switches back to stern police officer tone. "Shane, let's stop with all the honking though, okay? And" he continues, slowly putting his aviators back on, "try to be a little nicer to your sister." He hands Shane his license back and gives Sarah a smile.

"See you at practice," he says. "Unlike you, I can't change in my car, so maybe you can start organizing the kids, play catch with anyone who arrives early? I'm going to grab my truck and practice gear at the station right now."

Shane sounds relieved and cocky at the same time as he watches Dan recede in the side mirror.

"I knew he wasn't going to do anything. I wasn't even worried."

"You're so full of it," Sarah laughs. "You've been a *disaster* ever since you heard that siren. You're lucky Coach Dan was nice and didn't give you a ticket. Mom would have been pissed."

"Yeah, well Mom doesn't have to know, now does she Sarah?"

Sarah knows when to take advantage of an opportunity with her brother. "You're right, Mom doesn't need to know . . . if I can use you and a few of your buddies to help set up for the Enchantment dance."

Shane is so proud. "*Well* played Sarah! Who knew my little sister was already so diabolical? I'll bring guys to help at the dance, and you never tell mom about us getting pulled over. Deal?"

"Deal," Sarah laughs, "but you just better hope Coach Dan doesn't tell her."

Shane eases the Jeep back into traffic. "Wait, how well does Mom even know Coach Dan?"

"They've gotten to be pretty good friends, and Mom does seem kind of flirty around him. And I mean, in his uniform . . ." Sarah takes a long pause and finds her brother's eyes in the rearview mirror. "I just don't know if I'm ready for Mom to start liking someone new."

Shane has been dealing with his own angry feelings about his dad leaving. He takes a surprisingly mature approach with his sister. Shane has also been speaking with a therapist and he's able to use some of what he learned. "Flirty mom does sound gross to me, but it's been a few years now. All of our lives just need to move on, including moms," says Shane.

Sarah's listening but looking out the window now. "Maybe Mom's ready. I'm just not sure if I am."

Shane pulls into the entrance of Alta Vista Park. From above it would resemble an anthill, with a seemingly endless stream of minivans and SUVs dropping off and picking up kids for practices. Shane waits patiently as a red Ford pickup slowly backs out.

While the Jeep is stopped, Sarah grabs her backpack and jumps out. "Thanks for the ride bro, it was quite the little experience."

Shane doesn't acknowledge his sister's departure as he's already lost in his phone and has cranked up Ariana Grande.

Sarah walks from the parking lot to the T-ball field, remembering all the hours she has spent here over the years. When Shane played baseball here, she had to come to every game. Then there were all the times she volunteered in the snack bar, her early years of softball, and now Andrew's T-ball . . . Alta Vista Park has always meant fun times for her and her family; except not all of that family is still around.

Sarah reaches Field #1. Andrew's team is called The Ducks, because of their yellow hats and yellow shirts, but honestly, they look more like Minions trying to play baseball. Most of the kids are on the field playing some version of catch with one of their parents. Sarah pulls her glove out of the bag and throws her backpack on the ground in the dugout. She looks up and sees her Mom's blue Honda CRV pulling into the parking lot. The passenger door immediately flies open and Andrew bounds out, carrying his baseball glove, wearing a full Batman costume. He sees Sarah and sprints toward her, his cape flowing nicely behind him. When he reaches Sarah, she lifts him high into the air and gives him a big hug.

"What's up, Batman? Your costume looks fun!"

"Mom found it in my closet," he says. "Even the mask!"

"Wow! it looks great. I'd think you'd wear a baseball uniform to baseball practice, but I guess superhero works too."

Andrew, back on the ground and proud of his costume, runs in circles so that his cape dances in the breeze. The other Ducks run over, intrigued by the arrival of Batman to practice. Sarah is pretty sure this opens the door for other super heroes to attend practice in the coming weeks.

Kathrine arrives at the field with a bounce in her step. "I'll be back to pick you both up later," she tells Sarah. "Is Dan here?"

"Look behind you," smirks Sarah.

Kathrine turns around. Dan is pulling his T-shirt over his head while struggling to carry two bags of equipment toward the field. Kathrine walks to meet him.

Sarah gives a wry smile and exaggerates her sexy voice, purring. "Have a nice talk, Mom." Sarah's also thinking to herself, *this can't be good news for Shane.*

Kathrine smiles back at Sarah but ignores her comment, knowing full well that talking with her daughter about her social life is not a road she ever wants to go down. Sarah watches Coach Dan and her Mom smile and have a short conversation, as Kathrine heads back to her car.

Coach Dan enters the dugout area and empties the baseball equipment onto the ground. He whistles to all the Ducks, and soon he's surrounded by lots of yellow and a solo Batman. "Okay, kiddos, let's get warmed up. Leave your gloves here. I want all you Ducks to jog or fly down to the other backstop to get loose. Then run back here—and that includes you, Batman!" Coach

Dan extends his hand and gives some of the kid's high fives as they pass.

The team takes off in the general direction of the other backstop. A few of the parent's jog alongside, trying to encourage them while quacking. They might be called the Ducks, but it's more like herding sheep. Sarah and Coach Dan share a laugh as the kids take off running.

"Hey," he asks, "do you remember when I said I needed to talk to you in the hall at school?"

"Yeah, that's right, when you were with Stryker," she answers. "I'm so sorry, I totally forgot." Sarah is usually pretty responsible, and realizes she was a little distracted after meeting Stryker.

"That's okay. With your grandfather passing last week, and getting ready for the dance, I know things are busy." Coach Dan pauses for a second as he sees several late Ducks arriving to the field. "Actually, Stryker's little brother is going to practice with us today. They missed signups after moving here, but I told his mom the more the merrier at practice."

Sarah's been listening, but not really *listening*. She perks up and thinks. *This means there's a chance for a Stryker sighting at practices. And that—*

Coach Dan interrupts her thoughts. "Anyway, what I wanted to talk to you about was. . .well, your Mom and I have gotten to be pretty good friends. I'd like to ask her out on a date. I just wanted to check with you first to make sure it would be okay. I spend a lot of time around you at school and at practices. I wanted to make sure that you were comfortable with it."

Sarah knows exactly how her mom will respond if Dan asks her out. She's excited for her. But she also knows it would be her Mom's first date since dad left them. Sarah is not sure she's ready to deal with her own unsettled feelings about her parents. A bit perplexed, Sarah unclips her hair while immediately re-clipping it, for no apparent reason. She forces herself to look at Coach Dan and answer. "I . . . I don't think that's a good idea."

Coach Dan's eyebrows go up and his chin goes down. He clearly was not expecting that answer. "No?" he clarifies. "Do you mind if I ask why?"

"Well, it's 'no' just for now. With grandpa passing away, my mom is still a bit of an emotional nightmare. Your timing is not good. She has to go through Grandpa's paperwork, clothes, stuff like that. How about we talk again in a couple of weeks?"

"Okay, sure, a couple of weeks," he laughs, relieved. "Sounds good."

The Ducks, now heading back toward the dugout, are spread out all over the field. Some of them are still jogging, a few are walking, and a group led by Andrew—now without his Batman mask—are chasing a drone that some teenagers are flying above the outfield grass.

Coach Dan uses his loudest voice. "Ducks! C'mon, Let's go, Quack-Quack! Everyone please come in and grab your gloves. We'll split up and have some fun practicing, okay?"

With the help from some parents, Coach Dan and Sarah divide the kids into several groups. They spend the next forty-five minutes playing catch, learning positions, fielding grounders, and the most important baseball skill of all: leaving each other alone.

Coach Dan checks his classic Mickey Mouse watch as practice winds down. More parents and grandparents arrive as he calls the Ducks over and reaches his arm outward. All the kids jostle into a circle and race to stick their hands on top of Dan's. "Ducks on three," he yells.

Everyone counts, "One, two, three, *Ducks!*"

Sarah gives high fives to the kids as they head home. She sees her Mom walking toward the field, chatting with a few people, then realizes one of those people in the group is Stryker. Coach Dan's earlier conversation about dating her mom had fried her brain, and now she's caught off guard, again. Stryker's little brother is on the Ducks—*but which one is he?* Sarah scans the players, but before she can decide she sees Jason run over to Stryker and his mom. Stryker sees Sarah and waves hello before giving his little brother an affectionate kick on his butt as they head back to the parking lot.

Kathrine waves to some of the other parents as they're leaving, then she arrives in the dugout area. "Hey, sweetie," she says to Sarah. "I need to speak with Dan quickly, then we can head home."

"Sounds good!" says Sarah. "And I've got an interesting story to tell you on the ride home." Sarah scans the dugout area and the field, picking up Batman's mask, grabbing the rest of the bats and bases and packing them into Coach Dan's equipment bags. At one point she sees Dan and her mom having what looks like a *very* pleasant conversation.

Kathrine keeps giggling like a schoolgirl.

Andrew, who is tired after over-exerting himself during practice, is drinking Gatorade and playing games on Kathrine's phone.

Most of the families have left when Sarah notices two kids— one big, one small—running back toward the field from the parking lot. As they get closer, Sarah realizes it's Stryker and Jason.

As they jog up, Stryker asks, "Jason forgot his glove—have you seen it?"

Sarah hears Stryker's question but can only think about how good Stryker's arms look in his tight Fresno State football T-shirt, as she refocuses. "I put all the bats and balls away," she says, looking around the field and in the dugout. No glove. "Maybe he left it in the outfield where we were practicing?"

Jason's already peeled off to sit and watch Andrew play video games. Sarah and Stryker walk toward the outfield.

"This park is really nice," Stryker says, spinning in a slow circle while they walk. "In Fresno, I grew up playing at some places that were legit all dirt."

"Yeah these fields are pretty nice," Sarah agrees. "But you should see the fields up in Palos Verdes that actually overlook the ocean and Hermosa Beach has a softball complex that looks just like Fenway Park. It's so great there."

The sun is dipping below the oak trees that line the park as Sarah and Stryker continue to casually search the grass for the missing glove.

"It even has a 'Green Monster'?" Stryker asks.

"Totally," Sarah replies, "but I mean, it's a *lot* smaller!"

"Right on, that actually sounds pretty cool," Stryker laughs. "Ever since we moved, I've been trying to figure out school and baseball, so I don't really know my way around. I really haven't seen very much of the South Bay."

It's possible the sunset is influencing Sarah. She's feeling really good and she goes for it. "I'd be happy to show you around," she offers. "We have bikes at my house. Maybe one night we can ride down by the beach. There are plenty of places I can show you." The second she finishes, Sarah feels proud of herself for putting her feelings out there with Stryker—but the moment after that she starts to stress and immediately begins preparing herself for his possible rejection.

"Would you really do that?" He's pumped up. Grinning. "I would love that!"

"You have my number from—" they both say at once.

"Yeah, from the dance committee," Stryker finishes.

"I'll text you and we'll figure out a time that works?" says Sarah happily.

"Sweet, sounds great. We'll talk!" replies Stryker.

As they arrive in the dugout area, Coach Dan, still talking with Kathrine, looks up from his phone and says, "I just got a text from Anthony's mom. They've got two baseball gloves in their car. I assume that's what you're looking for?"

"Thanks, Coach!" says Stryker. "I'll tell my mom to call her and they can figure it out."

Andrew and Jason have turned off the video game on Kathrine's phone, a sure sign they're both ready to go home. Andrew wanders toward his mom and Jason runs to his older brother.

"Okay, another successful practice. Looks like we can all head home for the day," Coach Dan announces. "Thanks again for your help, Sarah."

"No worries," she says, grabbing her backpack while taking out some Chapstick from a zipped pocket and puts some on her lips. "C'mon, Andrew, let's go to the car," says Sarah.

Kathrine walks close to Sarah and in a sexy drawn out tone mimicking Stryker leans in quietly and says, "Sweet, sounds great, we'll talk."

Sarah shrugs playfully annoyed. "You're such a weirdo mom! And so not funny! How could you have even heard us from over there?"

Kathrine proudly replies, "Moms all have amazing hearing. It's part of the job."

Dan grabs the equipment bags as he and Kathrine get in their final goodbyes.

Kathrine catches up with Sarah and Andrew and appears to be in a pretty good mood.

The three Trout's climb in the car as Kathrine looks over her shoulder. "Did you have fun at practice, Batman?"

Andrew, still wearing several parts of a now very dirty Batman costume, answers in his deep Lego Batman voice, "Yes, Robin," as he buckles his seat belt with very tired eyes getting ready for one of his standard car naps.

Kathrine pulls out of the parking lot and onto Prospect Ave. She turns to Sarah pleasantly, "Sounds like *you've* had a busy day."

Sarah is sensing there's more to come and thinks this isn't a good sign.

After a dramatic pause, Kathrine continues, "I heard your brother got pulled over by the police today . . .?"

Sarah remembers her deal with Shane. She carefully considers her response, hoping it won't affect Shane and his buddies helping set up the dance. She decides to answer with a question of her own--already knowing the answer. "How would you even know that?"

"Ha!" Kathrine laughs. Surprised and maybe a little offended by the question, she lists the reasons on her fingers while continuing, "Let's see, *One*, it happened right in front of the high school where I work. *Two*, I was getting texts from people outside the school as it was happening. *Three*, I'm friends with the cop who pulled him over . . . and you ask, how would I know?!"

Sarah realizes that Shane is clearly on his own. Still, she tries to soften the blow to her mom. "Well, he didn't get a ticket or anything. Coach Dan was cool, and I *will* add that he does look sharp in that uniform."

Kathrine absorbs what Sarah just told her, ignoring the Dan comment and pauses for a few seconds, then speaks calmly, "Thank you, I will talk to Shane. But how did *your* day go today?"

"My day? It was good!" Sarah says. "I actually have a funny story to tell you," thinking back to her talk with Coach Dan.

"I actually have a funny story to tell you as well," Kathrine responds.

"You go first, Mom."

Kathrine, speaking with enthusiasm says, "I asked Dan out on a date, and he said yes."

"You *what?*" Sarah replies, flabbergasted. "Coach Dan asked me if he could ask you out on a date, and I told him no!"

"I know," Kathrine says. "Dan filled me in. It's nice that you're looking out for me, but your mother is a big girl. I can handle myself. Dan is a good guy, and plus it's just a *date*."

Apart from the hum of the road, the car is quiet until Andrew snorts loudly while falling asleep. Kathrine looks to her right and sees a few tears dripping down Sarah's cheek. "Oh sweetie, are you okay? What's going on?"

"I can't stop crying, that's what's going on. Is this normal?" Sarah says while trying to hold it together. She looks around the car for a tissue. Nothing. Would wiping her nose on her sweatshirt, like Andrew, help or hurt? "I know dad's not around anymore," Sarah tries, "but I guess in the back of my mind I hoped that he would come back one day. That we could be a family again." She wipes her eyes. "If you start dating Coach Dan, then the chance of that really happening goes away."

"I'm sorry you feel that way. Your dad leaving us was a horrible thing. But we're still a family, and I'm going to do everything I can to make it a great one."

Sarah takes some deep breaths and feels herself calming down. She knows her mom is mostly right—but that doesn't mean she can just snap her fingers and change her feelings.

Kathrine continues, "And honestly? Your dad made *his* choices. He just left his family, and he's not coming back—and frankly I don't *want* him back."

Kathrine slows down and pulls over to stop on the side of the road. She turns to Sarah. "I know *some* of the emotions you're feeling are from your grandfather passing. I feel them too. I know this is painful, and yes with everything that has gone on, crying is very normal. It will take time, but we're all in this together. I had a similar discussion with Shane. It might help if you two talk about it. I love you, sweetie." Kathrine grabs Sarah's hand and holds it gently.

Sarah manages a smile. "Thanks, Mom. I'm fine for now, and I love you too."

Kathrine pulls back into traffic and the drive home continues in silence. Eventually Kathrine tries to lighten the mood. "So, who was that boy you were helping after practice? He seemed nice."

"Oh, that's just Stryker. We go to school together," Sarah says. "Actually, I told him I would take him bike riding to show him around down by the beach. He just moved here."

Kathrine gets animated. She is proud of her daughter. "Well, good for you! Look at us—just two modern girls asking guys out on dates. Who has it better than us?"

Sarah reacts a little flustered. "Well it's not really a *date*. We're just riding bikes. I'm just showing him around."

Kathrine senses Sarah's stress and quickly moves off the subject. "Well good for you. I'm sure it will be fun!"

Sarah looks out the window, processing her thoughts out loud. "It is just bike riding, but . . . I guess it's also sort of a date. I need to text Kayla to see what she thinks. I bet she'll definitely say this is a date, which I guess isn't necessarily a bad thing." Sarah's cheeks turn a bit red and a shy grin grows on her face.

Kathrine just keeps driving as Andrew cutely snores. It will be interesting to see where this all leads.

Chapter 6

BROTHERLY LOVE

JOEY SMOAK HAS struggled to make his life work. His current foster family has done the best they can do, given a bad situation. He has his own room in their home, which is not always the case for foster kids. The small room looks exactly the same as it did the first day he moved in. No posters on the wall, and almost no personal items are displayed. The only decoration is a small tattered picture of Joey and his brother at the beach when they were little. When your life constantly changes, you have to move quickly.

A teenage boy finding his way through puberty with an inconsistent living situation can be extremely challenging. Joey and his foster parent Mick Martin enter the guidance counselor's office at South Redondo Beach High School right on time for his scheduled appointment. Joey has always struggled with school. He puts in the time and effort to study, but it usually ends up with him just staring at a page and zoning out. Joey has never been tested for Attention Deficit Disorder (ADD), as previous teachers had suggested.

"Nice to see you both. Please come in and sit down. Grab a water if you like," says Mr. Fairfield, one of the South Redondo High counselors. "I've been going through your file, Joey. I know you've attended quite a few schools in a short time, but at your age this is a crucial time for you to have some consistency. Statistics show that many kids with your history are likely to drop out of high school at this point. I don't want that to happen to you."

Mick turns to Joey and gives him a friendly pat on his leg and a reassuring smile, "We are going to get through this together."

Mr. Fairfield inputs some information into his computer and prints out a list of classes Joey would need to complete to graduate high school. He hands the list to Joey while he continues reading Joey's school history. "I see at Oakdale High School you were in a program for specialized computer coding. I've heard good things about their training. What was your experience there?"

Joey turns and squirms in his seat looking uncomfortable pulling the hair on his right eyebrow. "Yeah, they had a great program there covering a few different coding languages. I was doing really well." Joey pauses for a few seconds as his shoulders drop, "My living situation at the time fell apart. I had to be moved again. The new school didn't have much of a computer program," says Joey still fidgeting in his chair.

Mr. Fairfield listens to Joey's response while reading more about his history. "I keep seeing that you have trouble controlling your temper. Was that the reason your living situation fell apart when you were at Oakdale?" inquires Mr. Fairfield.

"It's all in the file." His voice rises. "I'm sure you already know the answer. Yes, I beat up another kid living at the house and got thrown out. You happy now?"

Mick Martin makes eye contact with Joey and speaks up. "Joey settle down, take it easy, Mr. Fairfield is here to help."

Mr. Fairfield leans forward in his chair. "Joey I'm sorry if I upset you, but I've been calling around for you. Bohemia High School in Santa Monica has a good coding program and they've informed me they have a spot for you if you're interested. The caveat is it involves you traveling to Santa Monica a few days a week."

Joey's face brightens up and his body language changes completely. "Wait, are you serious? That's great!"

Mick Martin quickly jumps into the conversation. "Unfortunately, that doesn't work for me and my wife Lorraine. We share one car. Joey has no way to get to Santa Monica during the day. The goal right now is to get him on track to attend class and get his diploma."

"I'm sure I could figure out how to take the buses to get there," says Joey sitting up straight in his chair optimistically.

Mick gets up from his chair agitated and starts pacing the office. "Mr. Fairfield and I discussed Bohemia High before this meeting. I told him it was very unrealistic for you to get there, but he brought it up anyway," says Mick, giving the evil eye to Mr. Fairfield. Mick continues, "Joey, I know this is disappointing for you, but the other school is too far. We just need to get you focused on going to class here, every day. Sign up for the correct classes that Mr. Fairfield has laid out for us and get you graduated. We can keep looking locally for other coding programs, but this one is not happening, I'm sorry."

Joey slumps down, all the optimism and confidence drain from his demeanor. He stands up defiantly looking at the others. "I knew this would be a waste of time. I don't even know why I came here. It's the same crap over and over again. You don't really want to help me; you can both go to hell!" Joey storms out of the office and into the hallway, leaving his updated class information behind.

Mr. Fairfield calls, "Joey, please come back!"

Joey is long gone.

"All we can do is keep trying with him. One step up, and two steps back sometimes. It's not easy," says Mick as he thanks Mr. Fairfield for his help and exits the meeting with Joey's class list.

* * *

Arriving home from Andrew's practice, Kathrine sees their house and smiles. It is light blue and taller than it is wide--just like so many other homes that line this area of Redondo Beach. Since buying the house thirteen years ago, Kathrine has not had to do much in the way of maintenance. The exterior paint is fading, due to the salty air and ocean breezes, but that is common for homes in the beach cities—and the recent backyard upgrades more than make up for a bit of faded paint. There are countless memories in this house, like the kids learning to walk on the wooden floors, the day Rick left for good, celebrating the holidays, and Kathrine's dad passing away. Whether the memories are happy, sad, or somewhere in between, taken together they remind her that this is her house. Her family's house. Like the house, the Trout's are a little weathered, a little windblown, but still standing strong. What's not to smile about?

Kathrine pulls into the driveway and frowns. One of her tall blue plastic garbage bins is tipped over, and trash is spilled across the grass. "Shane," she mutters. He talked about having some of his buddies over after school, which often results in some kind of mischief. "The Ventures" 60's classic surf music is blaring out of Shane's window from the backyard.

Sarah, unbuckling from the front seat, is always glad to see her older brother get in trouble, but she knows better than to show her emotions on her face. She gets out and helps a sleepy Andrew climb out of the backseat. "Andrew, do you ever *not* nap in the car?" she jokes. He's too groggy to joke back, so she just gives him a loving rub on his head.

Kathrine has stationed herself near the garbage. "Shane!" she yells. "Please come here!"

Sarah, hearing her mom on the way inside, flinches. "Mom, you're so loud. Just text him!"

Before Kathrine can pull out her phone, the backyard gate bangs open as Shane and Harry, one of Shane's surfing buddies, run out laughing.

"I know, Mom, I know," Shane says. "We heard you pull up and we're here to clean up. Me and Harry were playing a version of 'cornhole' using full bottles of water and trying to throw them in the open can from across the yard. But once we got a bottle in, we realized it was easier to just tip the can over to get the bottle back out."

Kathrine admits to herself that Shane's idea makes a certain amount of weird sense, and the boys *are* picking up the garbage. "Come on, bud," she prompts Andrew, who is standing beside the car like a zombie. As Kathrine heads inside, she leaves Shane and Harry playfully pushing each other. The boys are acting as if they were Superman and the trash was kryptonite.

Sarah, who has been eavesdropping on her older brother's situation, sees her mom and Andrew coming and holds open the front door for them. Grandpa Al was old-school, and he had always been clear about using good manners and being respectful. Grandpa Al had done a good job raising Kathrine and instilling these values into her, and in turn Kathrine had made sure Shane, Sarah, and Andrew were all well-mannered. Andrew is admittedly still a work in progress, but at least he's trying.

Kathrine walks into the kitchen carrying Andrew's baseball glove, hat, and hopefully all the elements of his Batman costume. Andrew, clearly wide awake now, scurries past her and into the playroom, where he vaults over the back of the couch and turns on the TV.

"Andrew, you're all dirty from practice," Kathrine calls. "Please try not to make a bigger mess. When Shane comes in, he's going to help you take a quick bath, then right after dinner, you're going to bed. You've run around so much today."

Andrew feeling rejuvenated after his short nap and couch gymnastics, "No, Mom, I'm watching Mulan. You said I could finish it after practice."

Kathrine glances at the TV from the kitchen and sees that Mulan is in the middle of her final fight scene. Since Andrew watches this movie almost every day, she's gotten to know it pretty well. "That's fine," she says, making a show of sighing. "Let's see if Mulan wins today and *then* your bath." Says Kathrine playfully.

Andrew replies very confidently, "She always wins." He flashes a bright smile and grabs a pillow with both arms, holding it tightly and snuggling into the couch cushions while watching Mulan leap up to a balcony and fight off the enemy soldiers once again.

Sarah has settled down at the kitchen table and is aimlessly thumbing through her phone. Her homework is waiting in her backpack, but she's had a long day and can't quite face it yet. Sarah's main hurdle is a Behavioral Psychology project she has not started. She is supposed to do something out of her comfort zone and write a report about it. But it has only been a few weeks since Grandpa Al's passing—and before that he was so sick—and all Sarah wants to do is get back in her comfort zone.

"Mom, I can't think of anything to do for my project, can you help?" says Sarah.

"I will come up with something. Let me think about it honey," says Kathrine. She can see Sarah getting teary-eyed again as she sits at the table. Guessing some of her daughter's emotions are rising to the surface, she crosses the kitchen to give her a hug. "It's just going to take time. I know it's been a rough couple of weeks."

"I just get sad thinking about Grandpa and how he's not here anymore," says Sarah. "I just . . I just *miss* him." Now she is sobbing, and Kathrine wraps her into an even tighter hug.

"It will be okay, sweetie, I promise," Kathrine says. "One day at a time."

Sarah takes some deep breaths and purposely wipes her runny nose on her mom's sweater. "Again, I'm crying!" she says with a hint of laughter.

Kathrine doesn't mind. She just keeps hugging her until she feels Sarah relax.

When she composes herself, Sarah pulls back and says, "I just don't want people to forget about him."

"Your grandfather touched too many people's hearts for that to happen," Kathrine assures her daughter. "And not just our family's. The four of us will always share our stories of him. That's how life works. The older you get, the easier it'll be for you to understand."

Sarah turns off her phone and looks like she's concentrating on the table.

Kathrine leaves her and heads toward the refrigerator to start pulling out the leftovers from a recent chicken teriyaki dinner. She preheats the oven as she puts the chicken and rice in a large cooking bowl.

Sarah looks up from the table passively and speaks. "Anyway," Sarah begins, "I think I figured it out. To honor grandpa, I'm seriously considering trying out as a pitcher for the boy's baseball team."

Kathrine bites back most of her instant excitement but still sounds engaged. "That would be wonderful if you decide to do that. Your grandfather would have been very proud of you, just like I am!" She hopes she has conveyed the right amount of excitement, because she does not want to freak out her daughter—or worse, be so excited that Sarah thinks it's not a good idea. Kids can be funny like that.

Kathrine is relieved when Sarah stands and walks to the island. She pulls her mom into a long, meaningful hug. Just as they both give a pleasant rub to each other's back, Shane comes in from the yard.

"I don't even *want* to know what's going on here," he deadpans.

Kathrine smiles and looks at him over the top of Sarah's head. "We're just having a mother-daughter moment, which reminds me... I'd like *you* to have a brother–brother moment and help Andrew take a quick bath when his show is over."

Shane makes an irritated face as he walks through the kitchen into the playroom. "I'll be in my room when Andrew is ready," he calls over his shoulder.

"Thank you, Shane," calls Kathrine as Sarah slowly releases from their embrace.

Sarah goes back to the kitchen table and sits. "I mean, I'm not really sure how tryouts for the baseball team even work?"

"I can talk to Dan and see what's involved," Kathrine says, as she pulls open the oven door and puts the Corning ware bowl of chicken and rice into the oven. "He *did* ask you about pitching on the team."

Girls playing baseball with boys is not a new phenomenon. As far back as the late 1800s, girls played on men's teams. Grandpa Al would share stories with Sarah about Lizzie Arlington, the first known woman who pitched in a men's baseball game on July 5, 1898, in front of fifteen hundred fans. Lizzie became the first woman paid to play in a professional men's game.

Grandpa Al also talked about Maud Nelson, a teammate of Lizzie Arlington. Maud played in both men's and women's baseball leagues, eventually becoming a manager, a scout, and even a team owner.

Girls have been playing baseball with the boys for more than one hundred years. During the 1940s when men were drafted to fight in the war, many baseball leagues had women play to keep baseball alive. This eventually led to a professional women's baseball league being created called the All-American Girls Professional Baseball League. The popular baseball movie *A League of Their Own* was based around this era. If you read about high school sports on the internet or in any local paper, you will find an occasional story of a girl who is successfully playing baseball on a boys' team.

Sarah starts to think about what would really be involved in this baseball tryout. "I'd need to get out and start pitching overhand, like every day, which is fine, but that doesn't even include having to deal with the boys. Some of them are so immature."

Kathrine agrees, but she is still excited by the idea. "We'll figure out how to get you ready for the tryout," she says. "And I know Dan won't put up with any of the boys bullying you or being disrespectful. *Plus*," Kathrine emphasizes, "I know you know how to stand up for yourself."

"Thanks to you, Mom," Sarah says. She is beaming with confidence after Kathrine's encouragement. "I definitely know to say something to a coach or teacher if there's an issue. Plus, Dylan and I are good friends. I know he'll have my back."

Kathrine stops preparing the salad for a long moment. She is composing her question carefully, so she doesn't screw it up. She decides to go for simple. "And Stryker?"

Sarah, who has just taken a swig from her Hydro Flask, sprays water all over the kitchen table. "Oh. My. God!" she says, wiping her chin. "I forgot Stryker is on the team! How could this happen?"

Kathrine is happy to see Sarah is still smiling, even if it is mixed with embarrassment. She tosses Sarah a kitchen towel to clean up the water.

Sarah decides to have some fun with her Stryker realizations. "All of a sudden, he's everywhere in my life: school, dance committee, Andrew's T-ball practices, and now baseball. If I didn't know any better, I'd say he's stalking me!"

Kathrine, laughing at Sarah, chimes in. "Or maybe you're stalking him."

"Ha ha," Sarah responds. "You're so not funny, Mom!"

Andrew walks into the kitchen. Kathrine glances up and sees Mulan still playing in the background. He really must be tired if he's ready for his bath before his movie is over. Andrew wanders toward Sarah, clutching his scruffy softie. When he reaches his big sister, he hops onto her lap and wraps his arms and his blanket around her and snuggles close.

Sarah and Kathrine look at each other, surprised.

With his head still buried in Sarah's sweatshirt, Andrew says sweetly, "You're just like Mulan."

Sarah holds Andrew even closer. She's feeling the love. "That's the most adorable thing you've ever said to me. I love you so much." Andrew gives a contented sigh, as Sarah squeezes him one last time. "You did a great job at practice today," she says, "which is why I think you still have a bath coming?"

Andrew immediately perks up. "Can you give me my bath?" He flashes a wry smile and glances toward the hallway.

"Of course," Sarah agrees. "I'm happy to give you a bath!"

Kathrine has been closely watching her children. "Andrew, what are you smiling about?" she asks. "Are you up to something?" Kathrine follows Andrew's gaze and catches a glimpse of Shane around the corner in the hallway. He's been watching and listening. "Shane what are you. . ." Ah—she figures it out. "Shane, get in here. And Andrew? Did Shane have you come in here to ask Sarah to give you a bath because he didn't want to?"

Andrew tries to look sheepish, but then breaks into a proud grin and says, "Yes! Shane gave me a bag of M&M's to do it!" Andrew takes the purple bag out of his pocket and holds it up high for all to see. "They're the *caramel* ones!"

Shane's laughing so hard he needs the kitchen wall to keep him upright. "Come on, Andrew, don't rat me out so quickly!"

Sarah is enjoying the scene until she realizes something. "Andrew, did Shane tell you to say that I was just like Mulan?" she asks with a disappointed voice.

Andrew hangs his head. His grin is replaced by genuine guilt. "Yes," he admits.

Shane only laughs louder. "I *knew* you would fall for that Mulan line! My plan worked perfectly. You were all set to give him the bath until Andrew's smile gave me away."

Sarah's a little annoyed and sad about the fake compliment, but there was no real damage done, and it was not Andrew's fault. "You're such a brat Shane. Nice try. I knew you were in the hall the whole time, but now that you're in the kitchen, isn't it time for you to give Andrew that bath *loser?*"

Shane is still extremely happy with himself. His little prank went off the rails, sure, but he still had fun. He heads out of the kitchen with one arm around Andrew and the other giving his kid brother a high five for the effort. "We almost had her, bro, and no way did she know I was in the hallway."

Kathrine turns to Sarah while grabbing the dinner plates out of the cabinet. "Your brother Shane can be entertaining at times."

Sarah is not seeing the humor quite yet. "That's the exact kind of thing that I'm worried about happening if I try out for the baseball team. When boys get together around girls, they don't know how to act. They all try to be funny but they're just big idiots. I don't know if it's worth it."

"Please don't confuse your brother acting like a goofball with how every other boy will treat you," Kathrine says, hoping she sounds wise and motherly. "What if I call Dan later tonight and tell him about you trying out for the team and about your concerns? I'm sure he'll be happy to hear you're interested, and he'll definitely make sure the team treats you right."

"That's fine. I'm just a little nervous," admits Sarah.

Kathrine puts her arms around Sarah and gives her a kiss on her forehead. "Everything will work out, honey. Grandpa would be very proud of you for trying to pitch."

"Thanks, Mom."

Kathrine, trying to lighten the mood, adds, "And I think you're just like Mulan, too!"

"Very funny," Sarah says sarcastically. "You may think Shane can be funny at times, but trust me, *you're* not." Sarah pulls her backpack onto the table and takes out some homework while Kathrine sets the table.

Looking at her daughter from time to time, Kathrine wonders; *Maybe there is a way she can get this Behavioral Psych project done and have a little fun playing baseball along the way. Sarah might just get her Mulan moment after all.*

Chapter 7

DRAMA

KATHRINE TROUT, OR Mrs. Trout to the students of South Redondo Beach High, has been a teacher at the high school for the last fifteen years. During her time there, she has forged many great relationships with numerous students, faculty, and staff alike. When Kathrine walks across the high school campus, it can take a while. On this day she is walking briskly with Kayla as they head over to the theater department to do a little research.

"Now I'm not really sure how this is going to work; so, please tell me," Kayla inquires.

"Sarah's project for her Behavioral Psych class is due on Friday. The topic is 'getting out of your comfort zone.' Sarah wants to try out for the baseball team but doesn't want to deal with how some of the boy's deal with a girl. I thought, with my theater background, we could take care of two things at once," explains Kathrine.

Kayla is a bit dazed and confused as Kathrine continues speaking.

"I've been running around, speaking with the teachers and coaches involved. The bottom line is that Sarah is going to dress like a boy for her class project for a few hours while trying out for the baseball team," says Kathrine.

"That actually sounds kind of fun, if not a bit involved," replies Kayla.

"Dressing like a boy can be fun for a couple of hours, but I doubt Sarah will want to be seen in public. She has no other plan for her school project, and I know she's trying to get her grade to an A in this class, so unless Sarah has some of her own ideas, this is the plan."

Kayla, a little dumbfounded with what she just heard, slows her walk. "OK, I have two questions. First, does Sarah know about this plan? And second, since when have you dressed like a boy?"

Kathrine, amused by Kayla's line of questioning, responds, "First, Sarah has no idea about the plan. That's where you come in as the 'friend' to help me with her. Second, I played a man in a college play, all made-up—mustache, glasses, prosthetics—and after one performance, we went to the mall still in costume. It was fun and very interesting. That is really where I got the idea for Sarah's project. I still have the paper."

"Ok, it all makes sense to me now. But I don't know about Sarah," says Kayla.

"I've recently shared this same story with Sarah about me dressing like a man, and she seemed into the story. But more importantly, she has no other plan for getting her project done. Sarah will realize that this is her best option. All she'll have to do is write a short paper about her experience; how people may have treated her differently as a guy and stuff like that."

Kayla, being a true friend, playfully suggests, "Or you could just give Sarah the paper you wrote."

Mrs. Trout pretends to be angry. "Kayla! That's cheating. I'm surprised at you," she says in a more serious tone, "and Sarah needs to learn things on her own."

Kayla says proudly, "Just watching out for my girl."

From the other side of the hallway, Mrs. Berz waves to Kathrine and Kayla as she exits a classroom into the frantic crowded hallway. "I have everything we need. Krista got me a bunch of great makeup from the TV station. I have a fake nose, wigs; we can create a monster!" Mrs. Berz excitedly shows her enthusiasm for

Sarah's project, which Sarah is still unaware will take place. "I'll be right back with all of it," she says.

Kathrine playfully turns to Kayla and says, "Now, our job is going to be to bring Mulan to life."

Kayla, laughing, says, "I'll admit this does sound like fun, as long as bringing Mulan to life doesn't involve ruining Sarah's!"

* * *

Sarah walks out of the girls' locker room in her practice gear, backpack hanging from her hand, feeling excited about the day ahead.

Today is the day each season when the baseball players at the high school face the girls pitching softball on the field. The exhibition is called *Strike Four*. The first year of the event, a baseball player struck out facing softball pitching and declared, 'striking out is bad enough, but striking out to a girl, it's like getting *Strike Four!*' and the name stuck.

This ritual started five years ago when Kali Bjorn, who was the star pitcher on the softball team, challenged the baseball team to face her while pitching softball. Softball pitching is done from a shorter distance compared to baseball. The ball is much bigger and is thrown across the plate underhand at very fast speeds requiring faster reaction times and it is nothing like the typical recreational, slow-pitch league your dad or family may play. The first year, Kali had a lot of strikeouts and gave up a few home runs but created a lot of enthusiasm and bonding between both teams. The day went so well that the coaches made it a regular event, which is why they are here today.

As Sarah approaches the field, she can see both teams are already well represented. On the third-base side, Mia and CeCe have their softball jerseys on and are sitting in their beach chairs, waiting for the show to begin and texting on their phones.

"Let's do this, girl! Please strike Dylan out; he's so cocky!" says Mia.

Sarah looks across the field to see several of the baseball players, including Stryker, just lying on the ground with their baseball bats in their hands, more resting than actually warming up. The other softball pitchers have late classes today, so Sarah is the only softball pitcher taking the mound.

Dylan yells from across the field, "I'm going deep today, girl."

Sarah responds confidently, "We'll see about that."

The pitching screen is located on the pitcher's mound. There is already a bucket of softballs behind it. The coaches were smart early on and have always had the softball pitcher pitch from the side of the screen. With so many players who weight lift year-round and the softball pitching mound being so much closer than the baseball mound, things can get dangerous. A hard line drive off the bat of a baseball player can seriously hurt any pitcher, and this unique event is supposed to be about having fun.

There's a small group of parents in the stands chatting. Out of the group walks Ruben Acevedo, whose son played on the school baseball team five years earlier when *Strike Four* first started. On that day, Mr. Acevedo was asked to umpire the contest and happily accepted the job. Little did he realize at that time he would be invited back every year to umpire this event.

Mr. Acevedo says, "Hello, Sarah. Once you warm up, let me know when you're ready, and we'll start. I was sorry to hear about your grandfather. My son took pitching lessons from him one summer. He was great to us, a real gentleman."

"Thank you for the kind words," replies Sarah. I usually need a lot of time to warm up, but pitching to these dudes, I won't need very much." Sarah, sounding a little more sarcastic says, "It's only baseball players."

A few other softball girls arrive and start making noise. "Let's go. Let's get this started; they're going down."

"Five minutes and I'll be ready thank you," says Sarah.

Coach Dan comes hustling out of the baseball locker room like a man who is running a little late. Coach Nevs from softball is teaching a class now, so Coach Dan is in charge.

"Sarah, I see you've met Mr. Acevedo. He's like the mayor of *Strike Four*," Coach Dan says as they both hug and laugh. He calls over the baseball players from their "stretching," as the group has now grown to eight players: Dylan, Stryker, Trevor, Joey, Teddy, Jack, Sean, and Ryan, with a few others running late. Coach Dan, sounding like an enthusiastic carnival barker, shouts, "Here we go! Eight baseball players will face Sarah for one at bat in *Strike Four*. The umpire will stand behind the mound. Let's see who is better on this day—the baseball boys or the softball girls. PLAY BALL!"

The group of softball girls sitting and standing around has now grown to twelve. Mia holds up a simple sign on cardboard paper that reads, "GO SARAH with AN H!!"

Sarah sees Mia's sign and walks over to give her a hug. Mia knows that one of Sarah's big pet peeves is when somebody spells her name wrong, without the letter "h" at the end. "Thank you. That's very sweet," says Sarah.

"I had fun making it. I even saw your mom and Kayla down there working on some project with Mrs. Berz," says Mia.

Sarah turns and starts walking toward the mound, focusing on the task at hand of striking out a bunch of cocky baseball players, but for a brief second thinks, *my mom and Kayla working on a project? What project? Must be something for the dance...*

Sarah reaches the mound and goes through the bucket, picking out some of the better softballs. Dylan and Jack are standing near the on-deck circle, swinging their bats, waiting to put their batting helmets on. Annemarie puts on her catcher's equipment and walks out to home plate.

"You know we go way back Sarah, but today I'm going to show you gals how it's done," says Dylan.

The baseball players start whooping it up and cheering loudly. The softball girls join in cheering for Sarah, trying to get her pumped up. Things are clearly starting to heat up. Sarah grins mischievously at Dylan as she gets ready for her first pitch.

The umpire yells out, "Batter up."

Dylan grins as he gets into the batter's box, adjusts his feet, and gets set. The smile on his face is replaced with a look of determination.

Annemarie squats behind home plate and gets ready to catch, before playfully telling Dylan, "Don't embarrass yourself, champ!"

Sarah gives a casual wave to all the softball girls from the mound. As the cheers get louder, Sarah steps up to the rubber to pitch.

She's smiling as she looks to Annemarie for a signal, which will mostly be for fastballs. Even though this is all for fun, Annemarie needs to know what type of pitch is coming for safety reasons.

Sarah winds up and throws her first pitch to Dylan—a high and tight fastball that makes Dylan stumble out of the batter's box while trying not to be hit for ball one. Both teams react with cheers and boos.

"So, it's going to be like that, Sarah? OK," says Dylan laughing.

Sarah smiles back, thinking, *high and tight to keep them honest.* Her next pitch is a low fastball. Dylan takes a big swing.

"Strike one!" shouts the umpire.

The softball girls burst into cheers while Mia yells, "He can't handle you, Sarah!"

Sarah steps up to the rubber again. Dylan gets set in the batter's box. The pitch. Sarah throws another low fastball.

Another big swing and a "Strike two!" calls the umpire.

"Dammit!" groans Dylan.

The cheers continue from the softball girls as the baseball boys sound more desperate with their encouragement.

Stryker yells, "Come on, Dylan; you got this!"

Sarah steps up to the rubber. The pitch. This, too, is a low fastball away. Dylan takes another big swing and misses.

"Strike three!"

The softball girls cheer as Dylan walks back to his dugout, hanging his head in defeat.

"Next victim, I mean next batter," Coach Dan yells with enthusiasm.

The next two batters have a similar ending to Dylan's. Jack strikes out while complaining about the umpire's wide strike zone, and Sean hits a soft pop-up that lands in the infield. The cheers, laughter, and enjoyment from the softball girls continue to grow after each at bat. Some of the baseball players are beginning to realize this could end poorly for them. Nobody likes being humiliated, especially boys by girls.

"You boys are kind of weak. Is this all you've got?" CeCe yells.

Stryker, who is swinging a bat while standing in the on-deck circle, bends over to pick up a helmet as the assumed next batter. He puts the helmet on and begins to walk up to bat.

Abruptly, out of the group of baseball players, an agitated Joey Smoak pushes his way through his teammates and declares, "I'm hitting."

Stryker pauses his walk as Joey quickly grabs a helmet and a bat and walks directly past him, slightly bumping Stryker as he gets to home plate. In an annoyed tone Stryker says, "Hey, man, I'm up. What's your problem?"

Joey, sounding equally annoyed, replies, "nobody laughs and disrespects us."

Stryker tries to reason with Joey's irrational behavior. "Relax, dude; this is just for fun."

Joey ignores Stryker as he gets to home plate and puts his batting helmet on. Joey is known as a big, strong power hitter.

Earlier this year Joey had an issue with campus security when they thought they saw him walking around inside the school late at night. Joey denied it, saying they had the wrong guy.

Nothing ever came of the incident. This morning, Coach Dan was notified by school administration that Joey would be transferring again, making this Friday his last day at South Redondo Beach High School. Coach Dan has had no issues with Joey and feels he is a good player.

Joey steps into the batter's box, looking very aggressive and focused.

Catcher Annemarie notices this and sarcastically asks, "Have a few too many coffees today, big guy?"

Joey glances at Annemarie in disgust but says nothing.

The umpire yells "batter up" as Sarah steps back on the rubber.

Sarah, having observed Joey's interaction with Stryker, can see he's pissed off, but thinks to herself, *That's not my problem.* Sarah's first pitch is a high fastball that Joey fouls off with a nice cut.

The baseball boys get excited from Joey's swing and start whooping it up louder than they have all day, sensing they need something good to happen soon.

Sarah steps to the rubber again, takes her softball windup, and unleashes a fastball that crosses a bit more of the plate than she would have liked. Joey sizes up the pitch well and takes a mighty swing. The ball heads up, up, it is high, it is far, and lands way over the centerfield fence and into the outdoor swimming pool area. Home Run.

The baseball players explode with cheering and excitement. The softball girls sit in silence as Joey, who is still posing and watching his home run, starts slowly jogging around the bases in his home-run trot. The baseball team's cheers get louder as the team stands by home plate, jumping up and down to greet Joey after his homer.

Sarah stands on the mound with her hands on her hips, watching Joey gloat while running the bases, and turns away in disgust.

As Joey crosses home plate, he yells out to Sarah, "no chick can ever get me out."

Both teams' fans let out a big "oooooooohhhhhhhhh" as the baseball boys keep high-fiving each other in their celebration.

Sarah is a bit insulted by the extended celebration and Joey's dumb remarks. She aggressively walks toward home plate and yells directly at Joey, "If you think you're so great, get up and bat again!"

The crowd lets out another loud "ooooooohhhhhhhh."

Coach Dan, observing from a distance, senses that this is not heading in the right direction and yells, "next batter."

The crowd quiets for a brief second. Joey grabs a bat and proudly yells, "I'll bat again; she can't get me out!"

"OK Joey, get up again," Coach Dan yells.

What had started as a nice, fun, playful event to promote team unity has now accelerated into a full-on "who's better: the boys or the girls" event. Clearly this was not the plan, but now that Sarah's in it, she's looking to win it.

Joey enters the batter's box for the second time and stands to the left side of the plate. Both the softball and baseball supporters are as loud and as animated as they've been the whole time.

The umpire yells again, "batter up," as Sarah approaches the pitching rubber.

Annemarie, who has been very sarcastic and entertaining while catching, now has a serious tone and is all business. "Let's get this guy, Sarah."

Sarah's first pitch is a slow changeup on the outside corner—a pitch that no batter has seen from Sarah today. Joey is fooled badly and takes a big swing for strike one. The softball team cheers erupt while the baseball team continues to root for and encourage Joey.

Joey is not looking as confident after his first strike but digs in again, nonetheless.

Sarah approaches the pitching rubber and throws her next pitch: another changeup away. Joey, who is now crowding the plate, jumps on the pitch but hits a line-drive foul down the first-base line for strike two.

Sarah gets ready for her next pitch. She thinks about what Grandpa Al used to tell her: *"Pitch high and inside to keep them honest."* Just like her first pitch to Dylan. She takes her windup and launches a fastball high and inside. The pitch gets away from her. It comes very close to Joey's head and drills him right in the back as he's turning away.

Joey loses his balance and awkwardly falls to the ground with his bat and helmet flying into the air.

The entire crowd lets out a large gasp before going into dead silence.

Annemarie quickly walks over to Joey to check on him, just as Joey jumps to his feet and charges toward Sarah on the pitching mound in a rage.

Annemarie reacts and chases Joey to the mound as the umpire lunges in to intercept Joey's charge to Sarah.

The umpire is holding Joey back with both arms as Joey screams, "I'm gonna get you, bitch! I'm gonna get you!"

Sarah, not backing down, yells back combatively, "Grow up; it was an accident, you got hit in the back. Stop your crying!"

All the baseball boys and softball girls run onto the field to break things up on the mound. A few of the baseball players help hold back Joey, whose shirt is ripped, and still very visibly pissed off at Sarah.

Coach Dan stands in the middle of it all and shouts, "That's it! We are done. *Strike Four* is over. Everybody back to school, back inside now!"

The girls head to one side of the field with Sarah while the boys head to the other side with Joey. Everyone is still a little shocked about what just occurred.

While being escorted away, Joey turns toward Sarah and yells in anger, "This isn't over!"

Coach Dan yells back aggressively, "Joey! Inside my office. Right now!"

Joey ignores Coach Dan and marches instead to the parking lot, angrily muttering to himself.

Coach Dan walks over to check on Sarah. "Are you OK? I know Joey can be a bit of a hothead, but I have never seen him lose it like that before. That was bizarre."

Sarah only now starts to absorb all that's occurred. "Wow, I'm just glad the umpire was there to step in because I don't know what would have happened if he wasn't there. I didn't mean to hit him. I was trying to strike him out. Joey was really out of control."

A few of the baseball players, including Stryker, come over to Sarah to check on her. Stryker gives Sarah a comforting pat on her back.

"That was unreal. I'm so sorry. Don't worry, though. I had your back, Sarah, and I was ready to step in if needed," says Dylan.

"Thanks, Dylan. You would have been needed; Joey was going ballistic!"

Dylan, now laughing, says, "Well the good news that came out of this little melee is that now nobody's talking about me striking out on four pitches."

Dylan gives Sarah a hug. "I gotta get going; great job out there today."

Stryker chimes in. "Yeah, me too; hang in there, Sarah," as they both jog off to the locker room.

Most of the softball girls have picked up their backpacks and take turns hugging Sarah and offering words of encouragement as they head out.

"Well that was a bit intense. Please text me if you need anything," says Annemarie.

Sarah picks up her backpack and starts heading into school when she sees Kayla and her mom walking to the field. Kayla jogs ahead as Kathrine goes to get an update from Dan.

"Are you OK? We just heard about the drama. Wasn't that the guy you texted me about who asked you out?" asks Kayla.

Sarah, a little more composed, "Yes, I'm fine. Things got out of hand quickly. It was actually very scary. And yes, Joey was that guy."

"I'm just glad you're OK," says Kayla as she puts her arm around her friend. "Apparently some guys don't handle rejection very well," suggests Kayla.

Sarah and Kayla start walking toward school. Kayla, with a wide grin on her face, says, "Come to the art department with me and your mom for a fun distraction. If you think *that* was crazy, just wait, because things are about to get *really weird*."

Sarah, still a little foggy from her confrontation, wonders aloud, "Wait, Kayla, what are you talking about?"

She is about to find out.

Chapter 8

LET'S RIDE

S ARAH FINISHES DIGGING through her shirt drawer to put on her white, slightly faded Enchantment Under the Sea dance T-shirt from two years ago. The shirt with the red lobster wearing trendy sunglasses, a backward baseball hat, and checkered board shorts was a big seller that year. Kathrine has helped chaperone the event for years, so getting a free T-shirt is always fun.

When it comes to the dance, one thing Sarah has learned from Mrs. Berz is "Promote! Promote! Promote!" Just getting the word out there in any form is great publicity for the upcoming dance. Sarah wears her shirt proudly as she turns and flops on her bed. For someone who is always busy, she is really good about relaxing and sleeping. It's a very simple plan: it starts with relaxing and quickly ends in sleeping--the end.

Sarah is replaying the last few hours and how the whole Joey Smoak altercation became a *thing* and how her mom put together her class project, which seems a bit convoluted and potentially embarrassing. But amidst all the drama, she can't stop thinking about Stryker comforting her by putting his hand on her back at softball. An active afternoon to say the least.

Then, Sarah looks at her phone to see a text from Stryker. This is the first time he's ever texted her. Sarah sits up immediately and starts flipping out. *What does he want? Something about the dance? Is he warning me about Joey Smoak?*

Sarah composes herself and looks at the phone to read the message: "Hey, what do you think about us going bike riding tonight? Crazy day. Let me know?"

Sarah takes a moment to absorb it all. *Oh my god, he wants to see me. Kayla said this would be considered a date; this is crazy!*

Sarah immediately texts Kayla and updates her. "Stryker texted me, wants to ride bikes tonight, FREAKING OUT!" Sarah mentally turns to "bike mode" and thinks about where their bikes are, and which ones are in working order. She texts her mom, who is also somewhere in the house, and gets an update on which bikes to use.

Sarah hears back from Kayla, "GREAT NEWS!! Try to relax, hang out, have fun, YOU GOT THIS!"

Sarah is a little calmer after hearing from Kayla and waits a few minutes while putting together her thoughts for her reply to Stryker. She comes up with: "Hey, yeah tonight works fine. How about six o'clock my house? We'll bike down toward the beach, my address is…" And send. Sarah thinks, *oh my God, this is really happening.*

Stryker stands in front of his bathroom mirror checking out his bike riding attire. He likes what he sees, but his *look* appears to be incomplete. "Mom, have you seen my sunglasses?" says Stryker loudly sounding stressed.

"I have them with your dad's glasses down by the door. I found them in a box in the garage. No idea how they ended up there."

Stryker happily grabs his glasses and puts them on top of his head as he sits on the couch waiting. "Can you take me to Sarah's now? I don't want to be late," says Stryker.

"Two minutes, and I'll be ready. I'm excited you have plans, and with your brothers T-ball coach. What a small world," his mom says.

"I'm not sure how that happened either," says Stryker smiling, "but Sarah was nice enough to offer to show me around, so I'll take it."

Stryker wipes some crumbs from his tight T-shirt as he exits his mom's car at Sarah's house. The small bag of Nacho Cheese Doritos he grabbed while heading out the door is long gone, only the pieces that missed his mouth are alive to tell about it.

His mom shouts, "I need to meet your father at eight-thirty, so I'll pick you up just before then," as he hustles out of the car.

Stryker is halfway across the lawn when the front door flies open and out bounds Shane with his two buddies Harry and Will. All of them are surprised to see someone standing right outside the door.

"Hey, uh, is Sarah home?" asks Stryker.

Shane, acting as a protective brother and the man of the house, asks, "And you are?"

"I'm Stryker. Sarah and I are going bike riding."

Harry chimes in quickly and loudly, goofing around, "Well, sounds like Sarah's got a date! Are you her new boy toy or something?"

Shane and his buddies have a good laugh as Stryker becomes a little embarrassed and sheepishly responds, "We're just friends."

"Friends for now!" Harry joyfully and loudly responds.

Harry and Will continue past Stryker. The boys enjoy laughing to themselves while Shane turns back to the house to tell Sarah she has a visitor.

Sarah, who had heard the talking and laughter going on outside, comes to the door and opens it. In a welcoming tone she says, "Hi Stryker; come on in."

Harry yells loudly for the world to hear, "Sarah, your boyfriend is here!"

Sarah ignores the comment, a little embarrassed, and holds the door open for Stryker as Shane turns to catch up to his buddies.

Sarah continues a bit annoyed, "Sorry about all of that. Shane's friends are idiots, just ignore them."

"That's OK. They were kind of funny. I had never met your brother before."

Sarah steals a quick second to look over Stryker. He's looking fit and tan, with a bright smile and a brown T-shirt that matches his dark eyes, as well as faded jeans, black Oakley sunglasses, and a sweatshirt tied around his waist. But the most important thing Sarah notices is the smell of his cologne. Sarah and Kayla had a long discussion about what it would be like when Stryker and Sarah had "bike riding" night.

Kayla's dating thoughts were: "If Stryker is wearing cologne, he definitely looks at this like a date. Otherwise, why would you put on cologne if you're just riding bikes with a friend," said Kayla. "Would you put on perfume if you and I were just going biking riding? Of course not! If he's wearing cologne, *you're in!*"

Sarah is happy about the significance of Stryker wearing cologne. She's guessing it's probably something like Axe; the staple of many young boys, including Shane. Sarah hopes he'll notice her Chanel perfume but knows that is not a strength of most teenage boys.

She briefly shows Stryker around the house. "This is a picture of my grandfather pitching for Kansas City. These are shots of Shane and me surfing."

"Great pictures," says Stryker.

Sarah hears her mom walking around upstairs. To move things along, she quietly heads Stryker out to the garage to get the bikes. She knows it will be much easier if they leave before her mom comes downstairs. She would have a bunch of lame questions for Stryker like "Where are you from?" and "How do you like Redondo?" So, leaving promptly keeps the night moving and is less embarrassing for everyone.

The two red and blue beach cruiser bikes Kathrine told Sarah to use were cleaned up and ready to go when they got to the garage. Sarah definitely noticed and made a mental note to thank her mom for that later. Most bike riding trips start out by trying to find an air pump and the elusive pin to inflate all the deflated tires.

The short bike ride down to the beach is uneventful. They take Pacific Avenue, which is perfectly lined with tall palm trees. The noise from a city work crew drilling on the side of the road makes it tough to hear.

"Did you live anywhere else besides Fresno?" shouts Sarah.

Stryker flicks at his ear while shaking his head, signaling he cannot hear.

Sarah shouts more loudly, "Almost there." Once they get down to the bike path near Second Street, they're able to quietly ride side by side.

For the daily sun worshipers, the day is definitely winding down. Most of the beach goers have moved on from their seventy-degree afternoon. The offshore breeze is blowing gently, and the sunset is twenty minutes away. Yes, it's another gorgeous evening in Redondo Beach.

Stryker speaks up in an excited tone, "I can't believe you've lived here all your life. It's so beautiful. I feel like I'm on vacation every day."

"My mom says if people come from all over the world to vacation in your town, then it must be a pretty great town," declares Sarah.

Sarah and Stryker ride slowly and calmly as the bike path is relatively quiet this evening. There are still a few skateboarders who look a little burnt from their party day at the beach, a handful of busy dog walkers, and some locals sitting on the strand wall waiting to see a great sunset. As far as Stryker and Sarah are concerned, however, it is just the two of them.

"Living in Fresno most of my life, I'm used to heat, heat, and more heat. Temperatures were in the hundreds almost all last summer. Our family and even our two dogs would get super dehydrated. The wind whipped up fields of dirt and things were really dry."

"Well that sounds like a good reason to move," says Sarah as they continue riding. Sarah glances at Stryker when he's not looking. She thinks, *this definitely feels like a date. And he looks so cute.*

Sarah chooses a path for them to ride toward the Hermosa Beach Pier, which the local chamber of commerce is happy to tell you is featured in the movie *La La Land.* There is a pretty good crowd of people fishing for halibut and perch from the pier. You can see cargo ships in the distance waiting for their turn to unload and enter the Port of Long Beach. Planes can be seen taking off over the ocean from Los Angeles International Airport. The waves are relatively small. Two young surfers are still working on how to stand up, at this point, unsuccessfully.

"So, you've been surfing all of your life?" asks Stryker.

"Yeah, it's been my thing. If the waves are good, I'm in. My Grandpa used to call me his little surfer girl."

"Nice. Surfer girl. I like the sound of that," says Stryker, smiling. "Surfers make it look so easy. Maybe I'll try it some time."

"Once you practice enough, it's easy. If you're serious I'd be happy to teach you. Just so you know, the ocean can be really cold this time of the year," explains Sarah.

"I didn't think about how cold the water can get. Maybe I'll just watch surfing for now and wait for warmer weather."

They stop their bikes along the pier railing in front of the "no bikes on pier" sign, each resting one hand on the rail for balance. Both of them are enjoying the developing sunset and the ocean view.

"That was pretty crazy today with Joey at the field. I really don't know him well. When he charged at you, I was stunned.

If the ump wasn't on the mound to stop him, I really don't know what he would have done to you," says Stryker.

Sarah smiling, says, "Well I'm glad I didn't have to find out. He seemed a bit out of control. I was shocked as well, but I would have gone down swinging." Sarah playfully mimics a martial art pose while on the bike. "I saw some of the videos people took, and to be honest, he did look disturbed."

Stryker continues, "Coach told us this is Joey's last week at Redondo. He thinks he's moving to Carson and starting school there next week. So, you won't have to see him."

"I'm not afraid to see him, but it will probably make things easier knowing that he's not around," replies Sarah.

Sarah and Stryker push their bikes away from the railing and start heading back toward the bike path. Sarah takes them riding in the direction of the aquarium on the Manhattan Beach Pier, as she points out all her favorite beach mansions. She tells Stryker about the local tours Shane gives people who come to visit them; places like Rocketship Park in Palos Verdes, the ocean coastline, and the Korean Bell of Friendship in San Pedro. They're all great places if he is ever interested in checking them out.

They continue biking into town and go past the softball complex, which is a replica of major league baseball stadiums, that Sarah told Stryker about previously. The sun has gone down for the day as they head back toward Redondo Beach. Sarah thinks that this so-called date has gone pretty well so far. They talked and bonded over family stories; Sarah spoke a little bit about her grandfather and Stryker talked about how hard it was for him to move to a new area. They touched on some of their favorite musicians, like Ed Sheeran, Marvel movies, and spoke about how to help keep the ocean clean.

They eventually stop in downtown Hermosa Beach, one of the neighboring towns that borders Redondo Beach. Hermosa is a similar town to Redondo, with a relaxed beach community, nice houses, plenty of beach volleyball courts, and surfing. They stop at Natalee's Delight, a local ice cream parlor that sells great-tasting ice cream, candy, cookies, and recently added acai bowls. There's a small seating area with stylish tables and chairs. Sarah has been coming here since she was a child. As they open and walk in the door, a cute little bell jingles, announcing their entrance. Sarah and Stryker head to the empty line at the counter.

Sarah begins to stress as she realizes she didn't bring any money on their ride. *If this is a date, is he supposed to pay? I need to offer money or say something.* Just as they get to the counter, Sarah feels something grabbing her leg. It's an excited, happy Andrew.

Sarah, a little surprised says, "Hey, buddy boy," as she gives him a big hug while using her hand to wipe some chocolate ice cream off his face. She is just about to ask Andrew who he is here with when she sees her mom and Coach Dan waving from a table while finishing their ice cream.

Coach Dan and Kathrine get up from the table with their trash and walk over to Sarah and Stryker. Kathrine, pleasantly surprised, says, "Hey sweetie," while hugging her. "I thought I would see you before you guys left. How is the bike ride?"

Sarah feeling a little uncomfortable with their impromptu meet says, "The bike ride is fun," as she turns to introduce her mom to Stryker. Sarah pauses briefly as she sees Stryker collecting his change from ordering their two strawberry shakes. Date night.

"This is Stryker," she says as he extends his hand to shake Kathrine's. Sarah continues, "And this is my little brother, Andrew, who you may have seen at T-ball practice."

Andrew begins acting all shy, clinging to Sarah's leg like it is home plate.

"And you know Coach Dan, since, well, he's your baseball coach," Sarah playfully adds.

Everyone shares a little laugh as Sarah and Stryker start walking toward an open table. Sarah, who has gotten comfortable with Dan from spending time with him while coaching Andrew, sarcastically says, "When do you ever do police work?"

Dan laughs at Sarah's comment as he, Kathrine, and Andrew start walking toward the exit door. Pulling down his sunglasses to the end of his nose and giving a sly smirk, Dan replies in a deep tone, "Maybe I'm working right now."

Sarah, a little surprised by the seriousness of Dan's answer, responds, "Ha ha, very funny," but briefly wonders to herself, *He's kidding, right?*

Stryker walks over to Kathrine before they exit. "It was nice meeting you Mrs. Trout."

Kathrine says, "Nice meeting you as well Stryker," and asks, "How do you like living in Redondo?"

Sarah does know her mother well.

"It's been a great month, I love it here," responds Stryker as he and Sarah sit down at a table.

Andrew waves goodbye while holding a giant lollipop he's swinging like a tennis racquet. Kathrine, in one efficient movement, takes the lollipop out of his hand and puts it directly back in its place on the shelf. She's good.

Sarah and Stryker sit back down as their shakes are brought over. A bit of quiet settles in for a moment before Stryker says, a little surprised, "Your mom is dating Coach Dan? I did not see that one coming!" as he laughs and takes a sip of his shake.

"The whole dating Coach Dan thing is brand new. This may even be the first time they have done something together, at least that I know of. I'm sure Andrew just thinks he's going out for ice cream with his baseball coach," laughs Sarah.

Stryker, smiling, says, "Look at them, just like us."

Sarah smiles back, a little embarrassed, realizing that Stryker is clearly being flirty with her. She is excited but a little taken aback by Stryker's flirtation and forwardness and quickly changes the subject.

"Trust me, I had no idea they were here or even doing anything. My mom who annoyingly texts me all day long did not seem to mention this. Coach Dan is a good guy, but at times it does feel a little weird."

"Well, how often do you see him?" asks Stryker. "I know you coach with him on Andrew's team."

"Well, that's true, but there are some things going on that may change all of that," says Sarah.

Now that Sarah's comfortable with her feelings that the night's going so well, she takes a leap of faith and decides to tell Stryker about her school project; dressing up as a guy while trying out as a pitcher for the baseball team.

Stryker, listening intently, laughing in parts, focusing on the gleam of Sarah's pretty blue eyes, responds, "That sounds incredible! I have that Behavioral Psych class second period, but my project on 'getting out of my comfort zone' is just about putting ketchup on a hot dog instead of mustard. Your paper sounds a lot better and a lot more fun than mine!"

They both share a laugh together.

"Yeah I agree; mine is a bit 'out there,' but it's due soon, and that's really all I have. I'm trying to get an A in that class. I've practiced pitching with Shane a few times this week. My arm feels good. The problem has been that my knuckleball moves a lot and can be hard to catch. Shane's been complaining a lot about chasing the balls and getting hit in his legs," says Sarah.

Stryker looks at his phone and sees his mom has already texted him about coming to pick him up at Sarah's. "We've got to go; my mom is on her way," says Stryker.

Heading out of the ice cream parlor, Sarah gives a wave goodbye to the staff, and says, "Thank you."

They get back on their bikes, and realize it is definitely dark out now, and biking home may be a bit challenging. Fortunately, the lights from the streetlamps provide enough light to see as they bike home. As they pull up to the back of Sarah's house,

Stryker can see his mom's car parked on the side street, waiting patiently with her lights on.

"Well that was a lot of fun. Thank you for getting the bikes and showing me around," says Stryker.

Sarah, much more comfortable with Stryker now, says, "That *was* fun, and thank you for buying the shakes."

They both stand outside the garage in a moment of awkward silence.

"Maybe we can do something again soon?" says Stryker.

"Yeah that sounds great. I would really like that," replies Sarah as she starts to feel a little nervous tingle.

Stryker stands closer to Sarah and starts to leave but pauses for second, looking directly at her; as their eyes meet, the moment is quiet.

A loud car horn is heard breaking their moment. Sarah and Stryker both turn to see Stryker's mom waving him toward their car to go. Mood killer.

"I gotta go," Stryker quickly says as he walks by Sarah, gently grabbing her arm, and holding it for an instant before he walks toward his car. As Stryker opens the car door, he lifts his head up and waves goodbye as she does the same.

Sarah turns around, a little giddy and excited. She takes her phone out to text Kayla and update her as she heads around the corner of the house to the front door. Sarah is startled by the sight of two people standing in the doorway hugging and kissing. Her first thought is it's Shane with one of his little "friends," but she immediately realizes it's not Shane but her mom and Coach Dan at the end of their date.

"This is so gross!" Sarah says as she heads up the steps and lets out a loud groan.

Kathrine and Dan relax from their embrace as both of them seem a little uncomfortable with being interrupted. Kathrine smiles, and asks Sarah as she walks by, "Did you have a good night, honey?"

Sarah, not hesitating, walks right past them, through the door, and pauses for a long second. She turns and responds sarcastically but with a sly grin, "Apparently not as good as yours!" as she closes the door behind her, and heads into the house.

Kathrine and Dan laugh it off while they embrace again. Kathrine is amused by her daughter's attitude.

Chapter 9
SHOWTIME

▞

MANY OF THE South Redondo Beach High School students are gone for the day on this foggy afternoon. With the school located near the ocean, it enjoys cooler temperatures in the fifties and sixties when the fog rolls in. Today is a good temperature for baseball tryouts and a great temperature for wearing theater makeup.

Over in the art department, Room 234, there is plenty of activity going on behind closed doors that's coming to a head. Ready or not.

Kayla, Sarah, Kathrine, and Mrs. Berz have come to the end of their journey preparing for Sarah's class project. With twenty minutes left before baseball tryouts begin, not everyone is happy.

"This looks ridiculous!" exclaims Sarah, annoyed and animated. "It's so obvious I'm not a guy; this is a huge mistake."

Mrs. Berz and Kathrine stand in silence with their arms crossed, ignoring Sarah's complaining while evaluating her new look.

"I like it! The hair stubble on your face really sells it. The new nose gives your face a wider look. The wig looks perfect and the makeup gives you a deep tan. You look handsome just like Shawn Mendez. It looks like you're ready to star in one of those Hollywood movies like *She's the Man*," says Mrs. Berz enthusiastically.

"I agree. You're just being dramatic, Sarah. Your brother's old clothes look good on you. Just try to speak with a deeper voice! I think you look great. I'm excited!" says Kathrine.

"They're right, Sarah; you look good! And on a side note, I'm impressed Mrs. Berz knows who Shawn Mendez is," adds Kayla.

Mrs. Berz proudly replies to Kayla, "I've still got some game."

Sarah looks in the mirror and confesses, "I thought this would be easier. It really feels weird looking in the mirror. My eyes are seeing a different person. It's freaking me out a little."

Kathrine, in a serious tone, exclaims, "Well, get the 'freaking out' part out of your system because you need to grab your glove and start heading out to baseball tryouts. We're all going to be there supporting you. The cooler weather will help with the makeup, so just try to relax and have fun; you're a good pitcher." Kathrine pauses with a devious look on her face. "And if things at tryouts go poorly, I am dating the coach."

Kathrine and Mrs. Berz both laugh heartily as they exchange fist bumps.

Sarah picks up her bag with her baseball glove in it and starts walking toward the door when she stops and asks, "Kayla, you have your phone to video and take pictures, right?"

"I've got everything! I'm on top of this. When this whole thing is over all you have to do is write the paper about your experience being a dude. I'm going to take a ton of pictures and lots of video. You'll definitely be getting that A," Kayla replies confidently.

Coach Dan is sitting alone in the dugout on the first-base side of the South Redondo Beach High baseball field. There is a small group of guys warming up for tryouts in the outfield. Coach Dan, who constantly has to juggle his schedule as a city police officer and a baseball coach, is enjoying the smell of the newly cut grass along with the peace and quiet. Coaching baseball has really been a savior for Dan. Seeing the rougher side of life as a cop on a daily basis can takes its toll, so being able to get outdoors and coach kids in baseball has been great for his state of mind. Now dating Kathrine has not hurt either. Kathrine raising a family on her own is something that Dan really respects. Plus, the fact that she's very confident and smart doesn't hurt either.

Coach Dan has run tryouts at many different levels for years. To educate himself, this year Dan sat in and watched the recent softball tryouts to see how Coach Nevs ran his operation. Dan is totally fine throwing criminals in jail for crimes they committed but cutting kids from the baseball team is something he has trouble doing. After the kids are let go, Coach Dan tries to keep some of them as part of the team either as statisticians, assistant managers, or announcers. It is the only part of coaching Dan doesn't care for.

As Dan sits and finishes his few minutes of calm, he can see a group of people exiting the school and heading out to the field. After a few seconds, he realizes that it's Kathrine walking out with Mrs. Berz and a couple of students. He rises off the bench in anticipation. A smile sweeps across his face as he realizes that Sarah is trying out for the team today dressed as a boy. He sees that the students with Kathrine are a girl and a boy.

Kathrine gives Dan a nice hug as she turns to introduce Mrs. Berz. Dan says hello and mentions that he and Lana had met once before, at a school holiday party. Kayla introduces herself to Coach Dan and says hello. Kathrine finds it surprising that Kayla and Coach Dan have never met before. Coach Dan turns his attention to the boy with them and immediately starts chuckling and covers his mouth to not draw attention.

"Oh, my goodness. Sarah, you look great; that is Sarah, right? You girls out did yourselves. Wow, it's actually hard for me to tell it's Sarah, and I know it's her!" Coach Dan says.

"This whole thing is weird," Sarah says in an uncomfortable tone. "The makeup feels caked on my face, the wig keeps shifting, and people are looking at me."

"No one is looking at you. You're just nervous. Everyone will just be focusing on their own tryout. Once you start running around, you'll relax and be fine," replies Kathrine.

Sarah takes her glove out and starts stretching in place while loosening up her arm.

"It looks like there are about seven guys trying out plus the guys already on the team helping with the drills. At some point I'll have you warm up on the side pitching. When we scrimmage, I'll have you take a turn pitching. Evan is going to catch for you. You can warm up with him facing the fence. I know your ball moves a lot. Fair warning, Evan won't be a big fan of chasing the balls he misses," shares Coach Dan.

Sarah acknowledges this comment with an affirmative nod. Some of the baseball players helping out arrive at the field, and Stryker is one of them.

A smiling Coach Dan playfully turns to Sarah and the others, "and what name will I be calling Sarah?"

"That's right, we need a name for her. Wait, I mean him. We never even thought about this," responds Kayla laughing.

Sarah mumbles to herself as this seems more involved than she ever could have imagined.

Mrs. Berz speaks up quickly, "Call her 'Marty' like Marty McFly in *Back to the Future*." Obviously, Mrs. Berz is still really obsessed with the movie, but it's as good a name as any.

"What kind of name is that—Marty!!" exclaims Sarah.

"One of my best friends growing up was Martin Golden, and we called him Marty all the time, so Marty works for me," Coach Dan chimes in.

"It's only for an hour or so; Marty it is," Kathrine adds.

"Marty, really? I guess that sounds better than being called McFly," Sarah says a little dazed.

Coach Dan quickly moves on and calls out to everyone trying out to come into the dugout. The four baseball players here to help out, including Dylan, also come inside with the group to listen.

Kathrine, Kayla, and Mrs. Berz find a place in the stands to watch. There are a few other parents of kids trying out for the team scattered around watching as well.

Kayla slowly walks away and heads closer to the field to get better pictures and video. She tries to act stealthy since anyone who knows her would be wondering why she is even there. Kayla is not friends with any of the guys trying out for the team, and she is not a big baseball fan either. Yet here she is, seeming extremely interested.

Coach Dan speaks to the group of kids. "We have seven guys trying out. Some of you I know and have seen play before, and for others this will be a first. We are going to run through some basic fielding drills with you for the first half hour. Then we'll scrimmage with live pitching. Besides Marty who else pitches?"

None of the guys trying out raise their hands as pitchers. Sarah stands there numb for a few seconds after being singled out as Marty and starts looking around. Sarah sees Stryker looking at her with a big smile on his face, but he looks away trying not to blow her cover.

Trevor, one of the regular baseball players helping, raises his hand as being a pitcher.

Coach Dan, a bit annoyed, replies, "Players who are *trying out* who pitch."

Some of the other baseball players laugh at Trevor as he puts his hand down from his momentary confusion.

Coach Dan instructs the players to head to the outfield to run through fielding drills. "Marty, do fielding for fifteen minutes then come in with Evan. He can warm you up before we scrimmage," explains Coach. "Evan, you should *definitely* put on the catcher's gear."

Sarah jogs to the outfield with the others. She begins to relax a bit, since no one has really taken any special interest in her. Just another dude trying out for the team. Sarah thinks to herself, *dressing up as a boy may have been a fun idea for my project, but trying out for the baseball team dressed as a boy is clearly not.*

The players trying out go through fielding drills and throw the ball to various bases. Very quickly Sarah realizes that most of the guys have stronger throwing arms than she does. They also seem to be a bit faster when chasing down fly balls as well. Sarah, who is very competitive even while being Marty, has settled into the pacing of the drills and is really pushing herself now.

It is Sarah's turn again, and Trevor, who is hitting fly balls to the group, hits a shallow fly ball to her. She runs in hard to catch the short fly ball and makes an exceptional sliding catch as she tumbles forward and hangs on to the ball.

A few of the players yell, "Nice catch, Marty" as she goes back to the group.

Josh, one the guys in her group, gives her a fist bump before asking, "Dude, what's up with your hair? It's all pushed to the side."

Sarah feels pretty good about the sliding catch but immediately starts to panic. She uses each hand to grab and adjust the wig without the use of a mirror. Sarah turns her back to Josh and starts walking away. *What was I thinking; this is so humiliating.*

Coach Dan, oblivious to Sarah's hair malfunction, yells to the outfield group, "Marty, come in and warm up."

Sarah could not be happier to get called away. She glances back over her shoulder and sees that Josh is very animated while talking to the others and pointing in her direction. Sarah hustles over to the bleachers to grab her backpack, acting like she needs something out of her bag.

Kathrine, Mrs. Berz, and Kayla all look on in horror as they can see Sarah's hairpiece has slid to the side and looks very out of place. Kathrine and Mrs. Berz immediately step down off the bleachers to help.

"Let's go to the restroom. We have pins; we can fix this quickly," says Mrs. Berz.

Sarah looks toward Coach Dan, who is busy instructing some of the groundskeepers about repairing a gopher hole near the dugout.

"OK, let's go; hurry," replies Sarah.

The three of them hustle to the outdoor concrete restroom. There is a brief pause as they figure out whether to go in the boys or girls restroom. Kathrine leads the group into the ladies' room, which is empty.

"This was a mistake. My wig is falling off my head; the guys are noticing," says a frustrated Sarah.

Kathrine and Mrs. Berz immediately go to work on Sarah like a NASCAR pit crew on race day. Kathrine works fast, using bobby pins to secure the hair in the back. Mrs. Berz is matting down the sides with special glue she got from Krista Stern at the television station.

"You're doing great; this will keep it secure," says Mrs. Berz.

"I don't feel like I'm doing great. The guys in my group know something is weird already," says Sarah exasperated.

Kathrine and Mrs. Berz both take a step back to look at her, while Sarah simultaneously looks in the severely scratched wall mirror to see for herself how she looks.

"You're doing great. Get back out there," reassures Kathrine.

Sarah takes one last glance in the mirror as she jogs out of the restroom and heads back to the field. Kayla gives Sarah a thumbs up as she jogs by to warm up pitching.

Evan, putting on the catcher's equipment, looks up to see Sarah jogging toward him. Evan, a little surprised says, "There you are. I couldn't find you. Coach says you throw a knuckleball! I've never caught a knuckleball, so this should be interesting."

Sarah thinks to herself; *I should give Evan some sort of response,* and replies in her deep Marty voice, "You're good."

Sarah warms up and throws close to thirty-five pitches on the side with Evan.

Evan was smart to take his coach's advice to catch with his back to the fence that separates the neighborhood houses. Evan only caught five of the first ten pitches that Sarah threw but was catching the darting, twisting pitches much better as she finished her warm-up throws.

Sarah thinks to herself that this is the first time she's ever pitched a baseball to a regular baseball catcher. She had pitched to her grandfather often in their backyard, but he never wore catcher's equipment, and he was always sitting on an empty softball bucket as a chair. It felt very different to her compared to softball, and she was trying to determine why. Hopefully, it wasn't because she knows a baseball can be hit a lot harder than a softball.

Evan gets up from his catching squat a little winded but feeling confident and starts walking toward Sarah. "That was so hard. You throw that knuckleball really well. I never knew where the ball was going. Good thing that fence was behind me."

"Thanks," responds Sarah in a deep tone, keeping things simple.

Coach Dan is pitching during the scrimmage when he sees Sarah is finished warming up and calls her and Evan over to the dugout. Sarah and Evan both sit and wait on the dugout bench. Evan is very happy to be resting.

"Two more batters, and then you're pitching, Marty," yells Coach Dan.

"Am I going to be catching?" asks Evan.

Coach Dan, with a sense of fun in his voice says, "You did so well warming her up and chasing all those balls, you might as well keep chasing them here!"

He gets a laugh from his fielders as Evan lets out an exasperated, "Oh, man." Evan clips his gear back on as his short break comes to an end.

Coach Dan realizes he just referred to Marty as a girl; fortunately, in the flow of the tryout, everyone just assumed he had a slip of the tongue.

One of the current players that has been helping out comes into the dugout and takes a seat next to Sarah. It's Stryker. He sits and bounces a baseball on the wooden bench, looking down at the ground, trying not to laugh and quietly says, "You'll do great out there, just throw strikes."

Sarah, keeping her head down as well while looking at the ground to avoid drawing attention, slowly starts smiling. "Yeah, well I'll be happy when this whole thing is over."

Their moment is quickly broken by the sound of Coach Dan yelling, "Marty, get out here to pitch. Evan, get behind the plate."

She grabs her glove and jogs out to the mound where Coach Dan is waiting.

"You hanging in there, kid?" Coach Dan asks.

"Barely," mumbles Sarah.

"Well, let's see how this goes. I was watching you warm up. Things looked pretty good. You're a good pitcher. Just try to relax and have fun, *Marty*." Coach Dan gives directions to some infielders then gives her a pat on the back as he heads into the dugout. Before sitting down, Coach Dan looks into the stands at Kathrine, who is sitting there with her fingers crossed while smiling back at him.

Sarah stands on the mound alone. She takes a few deep breaths to try to relax and also takes a look at the fielders to make sure they're ready. A part of her wonders if they already know that she's not who they think she is. Sarah sees her mom and Mrs. Berz still sitting in the mostly empty stands watching, but she doesn't see Kayla.

Evan jogs out to the mound from home plate and offers some words of encouragement to his pitcher. "I'm really tired, so please don't make me chase too many balls."

Sarah was hoping for something a little more positive and encouraging. It made her miss her softball catcher, Annemarie.

Evan slowly walks toward home plate as Sarah can now see Kayla standing behind the backstop, videoing for the project.

Tommy, one of the kids trying out for the team, is first to bat. Sarah cleans off the rubber with her foot and settles in. She winds up and throws the first pitch, which has good movement. Tommy swings and misses badly as the ball bounces off Evan's glove and rolls to the side for strike one.

"Evan, you have to move your body in front of these pitches to block them. The ball really moves," shouts Coach Dan.

"Tell me about it!" Evan yells back while retrieving the passed ball.

Sarah faces the first five batters and pitches very well. Aside from the occasional wild pitch, she strikes out three of the batters, walks one, and has one hit a lazy fly out to left.

Coach Dan jogs out to the mound to talk. "You're pitching great. I know your grandfather would be really proud of you right now, and I know your mom is as well. Let's have you face a few more batters, and we'll call it a day."

"Thank you, but my control needs to be better," Sarah says in her own voice to Coach Dan before he jogs back to the dugout.

Sarah is feeling very confident with her short stint of pitching success. A new batter approaches the batter's box before realizing he doesn't have a helmet and heads back to the dugout to grab one.

When Sarah steps off the mound for a moment to catch her breath, she notices a team of young softball girls walking past the dugout, dragging their softball bags, heading to their practice field. She briefly makes eye contact with some of the girls before turning her attention to the next batter who has returned to hit.

As the softball group goes by, one of the girls stops and yells loudly, "Sarah! Sarah!" and points toward the pitcher's mound, which draws everyone's attention both on and off the field.

All the players sitting on the bench turn around to see who is screaming and what all the yelling is about.

The young softball player, Kelli, sounds very excited and yells again, waving to the pitcher, "Sarah! Sarah!" She turns to her teammates, emphatically pointing and saying, "That's Sarah!"

Kelli's mom, one of the parents walking with the softball girls, turns to Kelli and says, "Kelli, that's a boys' team. That's not Sarah."

"That is Sarah. I'd know her anywhere!" responds Kelli sounding frustrated.

Sarah, like everyone else, has come to a complete stop while listening to Kelli, who is walking very close to the field. Sarah, still on the mound, turns away, bends over to retie her shoe, and thinks to herself, *this is so awkward, and poor Kelli.*

Some of the baseball players are now talking among themselves. Sarah assumes they are talking about her.

The young softball girls are moved along by their parents as they continue to their practice field. Kelli's mom puts her arm around her as they are walking away and tells her it's OK.

Kelli carries on a little teary-eyed, sniffling and walks with her head down when she somberly replies, "I know that was Sarah."

Kayla, who has been videoing the entire incident from behind the backstop, walks to the bleachers to sit with Kathrine and Mrs. Berz. All of them are a little stunned by what just occurred, but hopefully it will make for a very interesting project report.

Sarah, still a little rattled, realizes that most people think that was just some confused kid walking by when, in reality, it was the opposite. That was one really smart kid walking by. Sarah knows that when this little charade is over, she will make it right with little Kelli. But for now, she needs to compose herself and finish pitching. The day cannot get any worse, can it?

After a few more wild pitches, Evan is clearly wearing down. Sarah gets the batter on a hard ground out to the second baseman. The next batter up is Lance. Sarah has had a few classes with Lance, who was fielding in her group earlier and had seen the wig come out of place. Sarah wonders if Lance or anyone else is starting to put the pieces together. She knows the try out is almost over, but she is looking to finish up and end on a good note.

Sarah winds up and pitches. Lance hits the first pitch; it's a slow grounder between the pitcher and first base. Sarah breaks off the mound. The grounder gets past her before she can field it.

Ryan, one of the baseball players helping out, is playing first. He goes hard and far to his right and makes a nice diving stop on the ground ball.

Sarah, who had the whole play in front of her, continues running hard to cover first base.

The batter, Lance, who knows he has a chance to make the team from talks he's had with Coach Dan, is hustling hard toward first base.

Ryan scrambles to his knees, his hat flying, and makes an underhanded throw to first base. Sarah arrives at first base just as the throw gets there and steps on first. It also happens to be the exact moment that Lance arrives and steps on first base. Lance, who was running aggressively all the way, collides violently with Sarah, as both players tumble to the ground. The ball goes flying out of Sarah's glove. Both players, a little shaken, land on the ground facing each other. Players on the field come rushing over.

Sarah, who can handle the rough play, asks Lance, "Are you OK?"

"I'm fine, but...but what happened to your hair?" replies Lance a little confused.

Sarah, with a look of dismay, takes her hand to feel her head and realizes that it's just *her* hair and the wig is gone. In the rough collision, Sarah's wig and pins came flying off and landed on the ground next to them. A bunch of players who arrived there first all look confused.

"What the hell just happened?" asks Dylan.

Lance looks to his right and sees the wig and picks it up for all to see, while he's still sitting on the ground. Looking directly at Sarah, he inquisitively asks, "You're a girl?"

Sarah completely flustered and teary-eyed, gets to her feet. She takes the wig from Lance and runs toward the stands without speaking.

A bunch of the baseball players help Lance up and start to have a good laugh about what just occurred.

"Was that a chick? That whole thing was crazy," says Ryan.

"That wasn't just *any* chick, that was Sarah. Sarah Trout from softball. Believe me, wig or no wig, she struck a lot of you dudes out," says Dylan proudly.

"Sarah was dressing like a guy for her class project," adds Stryker.

Coach Dan arrives by first base and calls everyone in. He briefly confirms Stryker's comments about Sarah's class project but quickly jumps to baseball mode.

Sarah arrives at the bleachers where her mom, Kayla, and Mrs. Berz are sitting, all with a sympathetic look. "Please take me home right now! I need to get away from here. I looked like a fool."

"It's OK, honey, at least you pitched well!" says Kathrine as she tries to give her a hug.

Sarah ignores her mom as she starts walking quickly to the parking lot.

"I'll catch up to her," says Kayla reassuringly.

Kathrine and Mrs. Berz both give the "thumbs up" sign to Coach Dan as they follow the girls and head to the car.

Back on the field, the players get ready to finish the tryout. Dylan is laughing with some of his teammates and says, "Good thing I didn't have to get up. It would have been one more sport that Sarah Trout can strike me out in."

Coach Dan laughs at Dylan's remark, while grabbing his player list and marking a red check next to Sarah's name. In baseball you can never have too many pitchers.

Chapter 10
BAD IDEA

THE BLUE RANGE Rover turns slowly into the sparsely filled strip mall parking lot on Pacific Coast Highway in Hermosa Beach. On most mornings, you will see local workers and contractors getting their morning jolt and donut. Finding a parking spot can be challenging, but on this late Sunday afternoon, things are relatively quiet.

Five members of the South Redondo baseball team sit patiently in the Range Rover, waiting for their delivery at 7-Eleven. Stryker sits in the back seat, playing games on his phone, and says, "I definitely want to go tonight, but my mom's being a total pain. She says she's got things for me to do around the house, whatever the hell that means."

Jack, one of Redondo's better pitchers, sits in the passenger side of the front seat and says, "You'll be missing out, bro, this EDM festival in San Pedro is gonna be lit. It's right by the beach. My brother went last year and says it's a total scene."

Teddy, an outfielder and pitcher on the team who recently got his driver's license, is behind the wheel and adds, "I'm fired up; this is going to be an insane night!"

A beat-up brown Toyota pickup pulls into the lot with a blue surfboard sticking out the back. The truck quickly pulls in and comes to an abrupt halt in front of the 7-Eleven entrance.

The driver, a very tan young man with long blond hair, jumps out of the truck wearing plaid shorts with no shirt, no shoes; no problem. He enters the store while looking over at the parked blue Range Rover. A few minutes later, he exits the store carrying two large bags, one in each arm, and walks directly over to the Range Rover.

Teddy lowers the driver's side window. "You Connor?"

"Yep, I'm your guy. Sixty bucks, two Coors twelve packs," responds Connor.

Teddy opens the door, takes the beer from Connor, and hands him three twenties as their prearranged transaction is now complete. Connor takes his money without any discussion and walks back to his truck, jumps in, and drives out of the parking lot, likely on to his next delivery.

Ryan, one of the other baseball players in the car, an outfielder, says, "Sixty bucks! What a rip-off! Who is that dude?"

"He's a friend of my sister. He's got a fake ID. He buys beer for underage kids like us, but he charges for the service and makes money. Relax; I'm just happy we got all this beer. Now let's get this party started!" says Teddy.

* * *

The windows of the house are all open as the evening breeze is a welcome relief from the warmth of the day. Kathrine sits at the kitchen table sipping an iced tea, paying the monthly bills on her laptop. She has been hesitant for many years to pay her bills directly online, for obvious security reasons, but she has finally adjusted her thinking and finds paying the bills online much easier and efficient.

Andrew comes running into the kitchen looking for some attention, hops onto his mom's lap and gives her a big hug. Kathrine squeezes him back. "Hey buddy, are you getting ready for Shane to take you to baseball practice?"

Andrew nods his head in approval without really thinking about the question and asks his mom, "What are you doing?"

Kathrine smiles at Andrew and responds enthusiastically, "I'm paying the bills. We all work to make money, so we have nice things in our lives. You need a job to make money."

"Should I get a job? I want to make money!" says an interested Andrew.

"You're too young to work, Andrew. Just focus on having fun at school. Now go find your glove and tell Shane it's time to take you to practice. I'll be dropping Sarah off at practice a little later after we talk."

"Shane can help me make money," says Andrew as he hustles out of the kitchen.

Kathrine, proud of Andrew's fiscal attitude, responds, "Great, Shane can give you some ideas; now get ready!"

Sarah, dressed in frayed jean shorts and a plain pink top, comes down from upstairs and sits at the table with her mom. "What got Andrew all fired up? He's asking me about money."

Kathrine downplaying things replies, "Oh, he's just having fun. Shane is taking him to practice now, so we can talk."

Sarah waits, scrolling through social media on her phone, when she comes across a post on Stryker's feed from a Madison Everett. She talks about her family coming from Fresno to visit Stryker in Redondo Beach, and refers to him as "my boy." Sarah's shoulders slump as she tosses her phone face down on to the table trying not to overthink too much about what she just read.

"I'm so sorry about what occurred at the tryout. I know you didn't want to deal with all the boys, and I thought this would help. I was wrong, and I made a real mess of it," says Kathrine.

Sarah listens intently and replies, "I appreciate all the time you and Mrs. Berz spent on getting me ready. Looking back, it was fun before I had issues with the wig; only a few guys even posted about it, so I'm glad it's over. I'm pretty sure Kayla had the only video of it, and we deleted that part of the recording as soon as we got to the parking lot."

On the other side of the house, the front door quickly opens and closes loudly as Shane and Andrew head to practice. Kathrine looks out the kitchen window to see Andrew carrying some poster paper with his glove and Shane carrying a portable card table. Kathrine takes a second to think, *What are those two boys up to?* before quickly refocusing her attention to her discussion with Sarah.

"Well I'm glad. You still have to write your paper, but the good news that came out of this little project is you looked great pitching! I was very proud of you. Dan called to say you looked great pitching as well and wanted me to tell you that you have a spot on the team as a pitcher if you're interested."

Sarah's eyes widen as she blushes a little, and then her face breaks out into a wide grin after hearing the good news and the pleasant words from her mom. "Wait a minute, are you serious?! It was fun finally pitching in a *real* baseball game on a *real* baseball field, and striking guys out was obviously fun too." Sarah gets up from the table to grab a bottle of water from the refrigerator, opens it, takes a big sip, and sits back down. "Everything about the baseball stuff was great, but just being around all those guys and Stryker wasn't that comfortable for me. I'm going to tell Coach Dan thanks, but no thanks, to actually joining the baseball team. I'm happy to just play softball."

Kathrine sympathetically replies, "Are you sure honey? You pitched so well, and this is a huge accomplishment."

"I proved I could pitch to everyone else, but more importantly, I proved it to myself. I know that's what would have made Grandpa proud. I've given it a lot of thought and I'm really just happy playing softball with my girls."

Kathrine and Sarah both get up from the table and give each other a big hug. Kathrine leans her chin on the top of Sarah's head and says, "I'm happy when you're happy," as they continue their embrace. "Now, let's get you to Andrew's practice. Who knows what that boy could be up too?"

Sarah talks briefly about Stryker updates on the short drive to practice. Kathrine doesn't want to pry into Sarah's social life, but as a mom, she is definitely very interested. Sarah casually mentions that they have been texting more often, and that Stryker had texted her offering moral support after the "awkward" baseball tryout.

"Stryker hasn't attended any of the recent Enchantment Under the Sea meetings though and I don't know what that's about," says Sarah sounding disappointed. As they pull up to the fields, Sarah is hoping that Stryker will show up to pick up his brother from practice.

When Kathrine pulls into the Alta Vista parking lot, she can see that many team practices are already in full swing. As they approach Andrew's practice field, Kathrine cannot find Andrew.

"I don't see Andrew," says Kathrine. She can see Dan leading the players in baseball drills, but Andrew is not among them.

Sarah, a little confused, says, "I don't see him either. Is there a chance Shane took him to the wrong place?"

Kathrine reaches for her phone to determine Shane's location when their eyes become directed to a loud roar of laughter from behind the adjacent backstop. Sarah turns her head to see Shane laughing, standing next to a group of moms and some younger softball girls. Sarah points in Shane's direction as they exit the car and head to the practice field; still no Andrew sighting.

Kathrine walks closer to Shane and the others as more laughter can be heard. Shane is holding a bunch of dollar bills in his hand. When he sees his mom arrive, he says to her while laughing, "I told him he had to stop and go to practice, but he won't listen!"

Kathrine looks down to see her folding card table that Shane brought from the house. Sitting at the card table in a folding chair is Andrew. Kathrine wonders, *I have no idea where they got that chair from.*

"The plan was to make lemonade and sell it here, but that got too involved with buying cups and stuff. Once we got here, Andrew started taking his clothes off so he could sell them like at a yard sale. Being the good brother that I am, I quickly stopped that," Shane says laughing. "Then we came up with this."

Andrew is sitting cheerfully behind a big sign hung on the end of the table, obviously made with the help of his big brother, that reads "FREE KISSES 50 CENTS!" Andrew looks up and is very, very excited to see his mother and exclaims, "Look, Mom, I'm making money!"

The moms and young girls standing around all continue to have a good laugh. Andrew's smile beams brightly but is slightly obstructed by some fresh-smeared lipstick. Andrew says proudly and enthusiastically, "Most people buy two kisses. Shane is holding the money. We have ten dollars so far! Some people kiss me, and some people I kiss."

Kathrine, not wanting to "get into it" with Shane in front of all these people, looks over at him, giving him her best evil eye. "Andrew, I'm glad you're trying to make money, but tonight you're practicing baseball. I don't want you getting sick from other people's germs."

Andrew, still smiling and beaming, says, "I can't get sick! Shane told me to just wipe my mouth on my sweatshirt after each kiss."

Kathrine smiles toward Andrew but again glares sternly toward Shane and mumbles sarcastically, "That Shane is really something special."

One of the moms in the small crowd around the table hands Shane a dollar and bends over to give Andrew two kisses; one on each cheek, as all the young girls giggle and laugh while watching Andrew as he proudly accepts the kisses.

Kathrine finds some of this cute and funny but is a bit annoyed, "Well, I hate to ruin your little party Andrew, but you need to grab your glove and go to practice."

Andrew corrects his mom, "It's not a party, Mom. It's free kisses for fifty cents!"

"I got it, Andrew; now please go to practice. Sarah is out there already. I have to run a quick errand and then I'll be back," replies Kathrine. She peeks over at Shane as the group of Andrew fans heads off.

Shane sheepishly says, "I'll take all the stuff back to my car. I was heading out anyway."

Andrew crawls under the table to grab his glove, gives his mom a big hug, and says to Shane eagerly, "You can hold my twelve dollars!"

Shane quickly responds, "Nice try, Andrew; it's eleven dollars," as Andrew ignores Shane's response and sprints off, glove in hand, to his practice field.

* * *

The parked blue Range Rover fits in well among the beautiful lined streets of Palos Verdes. The ocean views from the cliffs are as breathtaking as any visit to Hawaii, but what's going on within the hills is not what the local tourism board is looking for.

The "pregame" is going well. There are crushed empty beer cans piling up on the floor in the back, and the fresh smell of beer has taken over the smell of overapplied cologne in the car. Electronic dance music is thumping loudly through the car's elaborate sound system.

Teddy chugs his beer and turns to the others, "I'm pretty buzzed right now; this show is going to be wild," as he cranks the music and the base thumps a little louder.

Dylan crushes his can and throws it on the pile. "*Bro,* you gonna be good driving to San Pedro? The road to get there can be pretty sketchy," shouts Dylan over the music as he pops open his next beer.

Teddy slurs his words, a little insulted, "Chill out, dude; you worry too much," as he takes another long drink. "I'm as cool as the backside of a pillow; a few more 'pulls,' and we're outta here."

The old coast road known as PV Drive has been pothole-ridden for years. The city has not made fixing these side roads a priority, but many drivers take it to avoid freeway traffic and to hopefully save time. Scenic ocean views combined with tight winding turns, however, makes it easy for a distracted driver to unfortunately end up off the road and in a dirt ditch or for the unlucky drivers, over the cliffs.

As the sun slowly starts to set, the baseball guys sit at a red light on PV Drive. The pounding music of Diplo can be heard and felt by all of the cars waiting for the light to turn green. Ryan announces to the full car, "I'm officially drunk, boys."

"Yeah, yeah, we all a bit buzzed bro," says Teddy as the light turns green and he guns the Range Rover toward the show.

* * *

Sarah organizes some of the kids for fielding drills, including Jason who is wearing his Iron Man costume to practice. It's like Halloween with baseball bats. Sarah sees Andrew running from his "money making" adventure, throwing his glove in the dugout and racing toward her in the infield. Sarah quickly yells to Andrew, "You need your glove, buddy!" Without missing a beat, Andrew makes a perfect loop while still running and circles back to the dugout to get his glove.

Sarah begins by throwing pop flies to the boys in her small group. She can tell these "Ducks" have been practicing at home; they've improved significantly since the year started. Andrew, who has always been a good little baseball player, is still buzzing from his successful "kissing business" and is not very focused for practice. The boys take turns catching the pop ups, but Andrew just keeps sprinting and falling on the grass.

Sarah is a bit impatient with her brother at this point and speaks in her big sister tone, "Andrew, please settle down; running and falling on the ground is not baseball. After you miss the ball you have to go get it and bring it back!"

Andrew, still being goofy, misses the next ball and throws his glove at it.

Sarah realizes she's fighting an uphill battle as all the young boys start to mimic Andrew's antics. It's hard for Sarah not to laugh as they are pretty entertaining. She decides to change the drill and has the boys lock hands in a small circle while dropping their gloves in the middle. Before Sarah can explain the drill, Coach Dan yells for Sarah and her Ducks to come in.

All the boys hear Coach Dan call for them, and like an old *Jackass* movie clip, the boys all bend over to pick up their gloves at the same time and bang their heads together hard. Sarah, part laughing, part concerned, asks, "Are you guys OK? You have to be more careful." Sarah slowly starts rubbing each of their heads.

A couple of sniffles and a few tears later, everybody seems good. The four boys start running toward Coach Dan while Sarah laughs to herself about what she just witnessed and takes a second to think to herself. *Who says baseball isn't fun?*

Coach Dan has the kids come to home plate so they can begin hitting drills off the batting tee. Sarah stands alone in the empty outfield, enjoying the calmness, and looks over toward the parking lot as parents begin arriving to watch the end of practice. She hopes that Stryker is one of those people. As more cars pull into the lot, however, still no Stryker. Sarah looks at her phone optimistically—no new texts. She can't help but think back to that social media post about his visitor coming and wonders if she was just being naive about Stryker.

As practice comes to a close, Coach Dan takes a few minutes privately with Sarah to discuss her decision not to pitch on the baseball team. Kathrine has already updated Dan on Sarah's decision so there wasn't much to say. "I know being around all these guys can be challenging, but if you ever change your mind, please let me know. I'll have a spot for you," he states.

"Thank you for all your help..." as she pauses for a moment. "*Marty* really appreciated it," Sarah says smiling.

Kathrine arrives back at the field to pick up the kids and goes to talk with Dan. Only two "Ducks" are still waiting for their rides; Stryker's brother Jason is one of them. Sarah feels a moment of disappointment as the other dad shows up and lets Coach Dan know that he'll be giving his son and Jason a ride home tonight. Coach Dan had already received a text getting the okay from Jason's mom.

Sarah and Andrew walk hand in hand to the parking lot. "So, I hear you made some money today!" laughs Sarah.

As a light goes on in Andrew's head, he exuberantly says, "My money. Shane has my money!"

Sarah playfully responds, "Let's race to the car; winner keeps the cash!" as Sarah holds Andrew back by the bottom of his shirt.

Sarah takes off running as the early leader, as Andrew shouts, "We'll see about that!" With all the determination of a boy who does not want to lose his eleven dollars, he sprints after his sister to the car.

* * *

Off in the distance, the wail of the police sirens can be heard as the first police car arrives on the scene. Two vehicles are pulled over to the side. The drivers standing in front of their cars are looking down into the ravine. As the officer walks toward them, he can see empty beer cans scattered across the ground. The first good Samaritan anxiously walks with the police officer to the edge and says, "This guy tried to swerve away from a bike rider who was on the wrong side of the road. The driver was flying and lost control of the car; it skidded and flipped over down the hill, it's hard to tell, but I think there's a bunch of people in that car...it's bad."

The officer looks down into the ravine and can see a blue Range Rover severely damaged; smoking, flipped over, propped up by trees and boulders about eighty feet down the hill. The officer scans the area to see if anyone was thrown from the vehicle and ended up on the rocks, or the ocean below. The officer quickly gets on his radio, "I need multiple ambulances immediately to the corner of PV Drive and Montauk Hwy; Possible fatalities."

Chapter 11
FALLOUT

SARAH AND KAYLA are up early on this sunny Monday morning in Redondo Beach. Sarah's already been surfing. The waves were a little disappointing—pretty small and no real shape. The surfing will have to wait for a better day. With the dance coming up this week, Sarah can only focus on all the work that needs to be done and, of course, Stryker. Kayla, still a bit sore from her early morning beach volleyball workout, is motivated and ready to go as she arrives at school. With coffee in hand, the girls are ready to put a dent in all the dance setup. The Enchantment Under the Sea dance is coming this Saturday.

"Well, we've only got a week to go. We have a lot of work in our future," says Kayla.

Sarah starts to pull out all the decorations from the boxes and lines them up on the floor. "I agree, but I'm excited for us to put our own spin on the dance." Sarah opens up the Enchantment Under the Sea floor plan and lays it out on the table. She begins listing the decorations they have and where they'll be displayed during the dance. Most people wouldn't even notice, but there is usually some "artsy" reason that a particular swordfish is hanging on the wall versus a large red Sea Dragon. "We have plenty of great stuff to choose from, and Mrs. Berz also said she bought some new items. I think she's got whales or something, plus the mermaid setup. So, I think we are good to go," continues Sarah.

Kayla playfully whispers to Sarah, "Quiet! I don't want others knowing about our mermaid stuff. I want it to be a surprise."

"We're the only two people in this room; it's still a surprise!" says Sarah laughing. She resumes logging the location information on the map and updates Kayla. "By the way, thanks for taking the pictures and video for my project. I got an A on my paper, which I needed super badly, so I guess the humiliation was worth it."

"You're funny; I was happy to do it," chuckles Kayla. She pivots to a new subject. "What's up with you and Stryker?"

Sarah ponders her answer for a few moments. "I guess we're fine. I know he was hanging out with Dylan and some of the baseball guys yesterday. I was hoping to see him at Andrew's practice, but he was a no-show. I sent him a text when I got home, but I didn't hear back from him. There was some post on social media about some girl coming here to visit him, but I've just tried to ignore all of that."

Kayla, being positive says, "It sounded like you guys had a good time when you rode bikes, and you both talked about getting together again, right?"

Before Sarah can respond, their attention is diverted to the classroom door. There's some loud talking going on outside the classroom before the door swings open and Shane walks in with Harry.

Shane obnoxiously shouts over to the girls, "Doesn't seem like you guys are working very hard," as he starts pulling decorations out of a box with no real purpose in mind. Harry joins in and picks up a newly painted dolphin display and starts rubbing it on his chest and kissing it.

Another example of why I don't want to play with the boys, Sarah thinks, as Harry keeps messing around with the dolphin decorations while trying to get laughs out of Shane.

Kayla looks at Harry and laughs. "The paint on that dolphin could still be wet; I'd check your shirt, genius," she says as Harry, with a look of panic, quickly starts brushing off his shirt with his hand and smears a small drop of blue paint that had landed on it.

Harry says loudly, "Aww, man, I'm suing this dolphin," as he takes a paper towel from Sarah and starts annoyingly wiping down his newly stained Coachella T-shirt. Harry gets a few laughs and now in a comedy role says, "This dolphin may need to get Flipper as his lawyer," as Shane gives a supportive chuckle to his friend.

Sarah turns her attention to her brother. "Can you focus for one minute, please. This Saturday night I need you and two of your friends here by four o'clock to help us with setup. You're also going to need to bring the ladder from home."

Shane looks and sounds a bit disheveled but very animatedly responds, "Four o'clock! There's no way; that's way too early. You said you needed help Saturday night. I repeat, you said you needed help Saturday night! Four o'clock is not Saturday *night*; it's Saturday afternoon! You're killing me over here."

Sarah finds her brother's little rant entertaining but ignores all the dramatics and tells him sternly, "You've done this before. You know how it works—four o'clock, three people—got it?"

"And why am I doing all this for you again? Mom already knows I got pulled over," says Shane looking at his phone and settling into a chair.

"One, because we're raising money to help keep the beaches and ocean clean, and I know that's something you care about. The second thing is I'm your little sister and I'm asking for your help."

"Well I guess those are reasons," says Shane calmly. He finishes texting and gets up from his chair. "All right, sis, I'm all set. Four guys at three o'clock Saturday. See you then."

Sarah is no longer listening to her brother, but Kayla, who is listening, jumps in, "You think you're so funny. It's three guys at four o'clock not the other way around."

Harry gives Shane a fist bump for his clever number play.

Shane gently pats his sister on her head as he's walking by and says, "And I'll bring the ladder."

Sarah looks up to her exiting brother. "Thank you. You can be a pain in my butt sometimes, but I do love you," she responds as the door closes. Sarah's not really sure if her brother heard her kind words, other than the pain in the butt comment.

"Your brother's a little wacky, but I'm happy he wants to help," pronounces Kayla.

There is a short knock on the classroom door as Sarah and Kayla both look at each other wondering who would bother to knock on the door as they answer in unison, "Come in."

Coach Dan walks into the room. Sarah and Kayla both look at each other a little confused as to why he would be down in the science area. Coach Dan says, "Hey, sorry to bother you, Sarah," as he curiously looks around at the dance decorations. "I saw Shane in the hallway, and he told me that you were in here."

Sarah notices a serious tone to Coach Dan that she has not seen very often.

"I have some bad news," declares Coach Dan, choking up a little and taking a few seconds pause before continuing. "There was a terrible car accident last night in Palos Verdes with some of the baseball guys and a few of them are in critical condition." The room has a deafening silence.

Sarah and Kayla both sit there with their hearts racing and a look of disbelief on their faces. All Sarah can respond is a mumbled "Oh my God."

Coach Dan gathers himself and continues, "I know you were very close with one of them, so I wanted to let you know."

Sarah's heart sinks to the floor as her mind starts bouncing off the walls when she remembers that Stryker was going out with the baseball boys yesterday.

"It's Dylan. He's having surgery as we speak. He has a concussion and some internal bleeding and is pretty banged up. They think he'll make a recovery, but you never know with these things. I was speaking with your mom, and she said you and Dylan were good friends," says Coach Dan.

Sarah is still in disbelief as the reality of the accident slowly begins to sink in. "This is so horrible, Poor Dylan."

"Word about the accident just started spreading early this morning. The other guys were Jack, Teddy, and Ryan. They're all lucky to still be alive. I spoke to the officer at the scene. Fortunately, they all had their seat belts on, but they all still have a long way to go."

Kayla, listening intently, speaks up, "What happened?"

"Well, Teddy was drinking and driving; speeding and making bad decisions. There were empty beer cans scattered everywhere. It almost got them all killed. They're in Torrance Memorial Hospital. I'm driving over there with Stryker, Evan, and some teachers. I'll keep your mom updated on how the visit goes. I'm sorry." Coach Dan immediately turns around and heads out the door.

Kayla and Sarah look at each other—Kayla is crying. "I have classes with Teddy and Jack. I can't believe this," says Kayla as she wipes some tears from her eyes. "When he said it was someone you knew, I for sure thought he was going to say Stryker."

"I did too. I'm happy nothing happened to him, but I feel so bad for Dylan and the others. I just can't believe this happened. His mom must be a mess," Sarah somberly replies.

Kayla and Sarah just sit there, absorbing all the information they've received in the last few minutes. They both look at their phones to see lots of new texts. Neither of them feels much like working now.

Sarah lets Kayla know, "My mom's been trying to get a hold of me, and I have texts from Stryker and some softball girls. They're all talking about going to the hospital after school," as she continues to scroll thought her messages. The science room door flies open once again as if it were a busy waiting room at a doctor's office.

"Mom? What are you doing here?" asks Sarah as Kathrine boldly strides in the room and gives Sarah and Kayla a big, consoling hug.

"I just spoke with Dan. I feel so horrible about what happened to those boys. Their poor parents. I can't imagine," Kathrine pauses, "You heard they were drinking?"

Sarah and Kayla answer in unison, "Yes."

Kathrine says with an emotional plea, "We really need to talk about this tonight at home. Those kids could be dead! And all because they wanted to drink. This is why I worry about your brother driving; all it takes is one bad decision."

Sarah and Kayla are numbly listening in silence until Sarah replies, "Well I've never heard Shane talk about wanting to drink."

"As you get older and turn twenty-one, plenty of people decide to drink. It's drinking and driving that's the issue at any age." Kathrine pauses, and continues, "Teddy had just gotten his license. He wasn't even supposed to have other people in his car, but he's speeding and drinking." Kathrine slowly turns to leave. "I'm going to the hospital after school if you want to come with me. Just to keep you both prepared, seeing your friends in the hospital will not be pleasant. We aren't even sure if we will be allowed to go see them."

"I don't do well around hospitals, so I'll probably just stay here and get stuff done on the dance, but Sarah you should go," utters Kayla.

"All right I'll go with you, Mom; just text me when you're ready."

Stryker hadn't given it much thought before but driving in a car with a bunch of your teachers was a little weird and unsettling. Listening to teachers talk about how their lawns look or their golf game shouldn't be an issue, but when your geometry teacher is talking about playing video games, it's a bit bizarre.

Coach Dan is driving and sounding like the police officer that he is asks, "Stryker, what can you tell me about the boys last night?"

"Not very much. I know they were going to a concert."

Coach Dan sternly replies, "That's the wrong answer. I know you were with them when they bought the beer. I know you don't want to snitch on your friends, but I can get all the information I need soon on my own; you can just save me some time."

Stryker feels stressed about his situation but concedes, "They got the beer from a friend of Teddy's sister. After that I got dropped off at home. My mom didn't want me going to the concert."

"Little decisions can change the world; your mom may have saved your life last night," vocalizes Coach Dan.

Stryker, sounding very thankful, replies, "Trust me, that's all I've thought about."

"They just need to get through the next few days. It's not going to be easy, and their recovery will be long," remarks Coach Dan.

As they arrive at the hospital main entrance, Dan drops off all of his passengers before driving the car into the visitor's parking lot. While searching for an open spot, besides his players health concerns, Coach Dan's mind starts to consider what his baseball team will look like for the upcoming Enchantment Under the Sea tournament this weekend. Chances are none of these kids will be out of the hospital for weeks. Losing four guys from the team, two who are regular pitchers, is going to make it tough to field a competitive team.

After school, Sarah and her mom head out of the high school parking lot for the short drive over to Torrance Hospital. Kathrine shares her thoughts with Sarah about her discussions with Shane surrounding drinking and driving. Kathrine explains, "I told your brother he doesn't have to ever drink but when he's ready to drink to come see me. That way we can figure out a way to do it in a controlled setting, so he doesn't feel like he has to go behind my back. You kid's definitely can't be drinking and driving."

Sarah listens to her mom's rant. She is slightly annoyed that her mom is turning this into a lesson but decides to just accept it; understanding that her mom is upset and worried.

"Stryker texted me earlier that he was almost in the car with them last night, but his mom wanted him home, so he didn't go to the concert," shares Sarah.

"That's one smart mom. I need to talk with her," Kathrine says.

Kathrine and Sarah glance around the fresh-looking hospital lobby to locate the elevators. They see a large group of people from the high school standing in a group talking; Stryker and Coach Dan are among them. The mood of the group is very consoling, with lots of hugs and lots of tears.

Coach Dan breaks away from the group and walks over to Kathrine and Sarah, giving Kathrine a long embrace. "The doctors said they don't want anyone else visiting for a few hours because the boys all need rest. They're all still in shock and disoriented; it hasn't even been twenty-four hours since the accident," he says.

"What have the doctors said about their injuries?" Kathrine asks as she sits down on an empty cushion.

"Teddy and Jack are still in critical condition, but stable. They both have concussions and major damage to their backs. Dylan also has a concussion and shattered both of his legs. Ryan broke his collarbone, but besides a few other bumps and bruises, seems to be OK. All of their parents are upstairs. It's a really emotional scene, but they're all grateful that their kids are still alive."

"Thank goodness." Kathrine sounds relieved at the news.

Stryker comes over to Sarah and her mom and embraces both of them. "I was upstairs for a little while. It's not a pretty picture. I had to leave after a few minutes." Stryker reaches into his back pocket and pulls out his phone to show a handful of pictures Jack's dad took at the scene. "The car is totaled; it could have easily slid down the cliff and ended up in the ocean," he says as he swipes through the photos.

As Kathrine and Sarah slowly look through pictures, Kathrine turns to Stryker and says sternly, "I hope you've learned something from all of this."

Sarah, a little surprised by her mom's aggressive tone, loudly moans, "Mom!"

Stryker, animated, says, "It's OK. It's OK. My mom read me the riot act already. I won't be drinking anytime soon, if ever!"

After speaking with some of the parents, Dan rejoins Kathrine and the others. "We can't see any of the kids till later tonight, so I'm going to head out of here; I suggest you guys do the same." Coach Dan tries to make the tone a little bit lighter, "Unless Sarah likes hanging out at hospitals."

Sarah, who has gotten much more comfortable with Coach Dan being around, turns and gives him a friendly punch to the arm for his silly comment.

And Coach Dan follows it with, "I hear the cafeteria here does a nice brunch."

Sarah gets in her goodbyes to Stryker, and they hug again.

"I'm going to head home, and Dan is going to stop by the house. Why don't you come home with me, Sarah; Andrew will be happy to see you," says Kathrine.

Sarah checks her phone and sees that Coach Nevs cancelled softball practice today with all the issues and commotion surrounding the car accident. Sarah tells her mom, "I'll come home with you, but I may go back to school later to help Kayla with dance stuff."

The drive home is very quiet. Sarah and Kathrine are both thinking about what just transpired. Kathrine, as a loving mother worries about her children drinking and driving, realizes the Herculean task she needs to try to complete. There is just so much to teach her kids so that they can make good decisions. She feels sympathy for what the other parents must be going through with their children in the hospital. Meanwhile, Sarah's mind wanders, *What are they going to do about missing school? Will they just drop out or repeat a year? Will Dylan even walk again?* There's so much unknown here, things appear to be a huge mess.

Mother and daughter enter the house to find Shane and Andrew sitting quietly at the kitchen table. Shane is eating some tacos from his favorite Mexican restaurant in the South Bay, Taco Bell. Andrew is working on math problems out of a paper workbook called "Skool's Kool" that his brother and sister have both used through the years.

Kathrine drops her bag and keys on the counter. "How are my two favorite boys doing?" she asks as she walks over and kisses both boys on the head. Andrew focuses on his math problems and doesn't move.

Shane waits to finish the food in his mouth, wraps up his garbage, and throws it in the trash before responding, "How was the hospital?"

"As good as can be expected. Those boys are all just lucky to be alive," Kathrine replies solemnly.

Shane walks out of the kitchen heading upstairs to his bedroom. Andrew sees Shane leave and quickly grabs his book and follows him up the stairs.

"Andrew, don't you want to do your math down here?" asks Kathrine, looking to give Shane a little peace and quiet.

Shane yells from upstairs, "He's fine up here; he's watching me play Madden."

Kathrine mumbles with a defeatist tone to no one in particular, "What about the math?"

Sarah looks into the open refrigerator, trying to determine what direction, "healthy," or "junk food," to go in for her meal. She grabs a handful of blueberries and turns to a knock on the kitchen screen door.

"Hey, it's Coach Dan," announces Sarah as he enters the house. She leans in toward her mom with a smirk on her face and whispers, *"Your third favorite boy."*

Kathrine gives Sarah a sarcastic "very funny" for her witty observation but quickly ignores her comment as she walks over to hug Dan.

Sarah observes her mom and Dan and thinks them dating has not been an issue. Her mom seems happy when she is with him, and it hasn't felt awkward when Coach Dan has been around. She surmises that this is a good thing.

"I know you're going to think I'm a big weirdo, but I asked Dan to come by to have a quick conversation with you about drinking and driving from a cop's perspective. He has seen lots of horrible accident scenes from drunk drivers that have ruined families for life. Dan was nice enough to have a quick conversation with Shane earlier today, and I just thought it would be good for you to hear," states Kathrine.

"Well you are a big weirdo," replies Sarah. She is slightly frustrated that her mom doesn't think the terrible condition her friends are in is enough of a lesson, but Sarah says "Sure, let's talk" as she wonders why Shane hadn't mentioned anything about his talk with Dan.

Dan sits at the table and pulls out his laptop from the bag that is already opened to his department's drunk driving website. "This is going to be really quick. I know you're already familiar with most of these things, but just talking about them for a few minutes will help, even if you're not old enough to drive yet."

Sarah adjusts herself in the chair to get comfortable, expecting a lengthy sermon.

Coach Dan, in his professional cop voice, begins, "Never get in a car with a drunk driver, no matter how many times they tell you they're 'fine.' Drunk people never think they're impaired. Recent statistics show that 17 percent of high school students have driven with a teenage driver who had been drinking in the last month. You can take their keys away. You can text any ride sharing service to get home, or you can text your mom or brother," Dan pauses smiling "your *older* brother."

As he's speaking, Dan is clicking through the website screens showing Sarah pictures of auto accidents that involved teenagers. "The police have a program where on weekends you can call an 800 number and volunteers from a veteran's group will drive you home, no questions asked, and it's all free. We'd rather see kids get home safely than worry about getting in trouble. If you see someone you think is driving drunk or erratically call 911 and give the police the information. We want to keep people alive."

Dan continues clicking through crash site photos, next showing a red Toyota pickup truck that had crashed into the side of a freeway wall with its roof torn off from the immense impact. "Just remember, you're at the age now where there are going to be friends of yours who start underage drinking." Dan pauses and takes a sip of his water. "Before a football game or a dance or just hanging out by the beach, you probably already know some kids who drink. I'm just telling you it's OK not to drink. I don't want to get into it, but like your mom was saying, I've seen many horrible deaths that revolved around people drinking and driving You've just seen these pictures. It's not pretty!"

Sarah squirms in her seat to readjust herself just as she realizes Coach Dan's talk is over.

"I told you I'd make it quick," Dan confirms as he closes his laptop and slides it back into the bag.

"Those pictures were horrible but thank you. I really have no interest in drinking," responds Sarah.

"I'm not worried about you, Sarah, but if you see things with friends or other people, don't be afraid to say something or call for help," suggests Coach Dan.

"Got it," says Sarah as she gets up from the table to put her empty cup in the sink, hoping to sneak away to her room and avoid any more of these discussions.

"I actually have one more thing, Sarah, if you have a second," says Coach Dan.

"Sure, what's up?"

"You may find what I have to say right now a little confusing, but the school's athletic director called and asked me if we were still interested in playing in the Enchantment baseball tournament. My first thought was to just forfeit the games, but Teddy and Jack's parents both came to me to say the boys would want the team to play in the tournament. This tournament has a long-respected history, and the parents admitted that, honestly, they thought it would be a nice distraction from all the sadness that's going on," explains Coach Dan.

Kathrine settles into her chair while peeking over toward Sarah with a wry smile.

"*Sooo*," Dan pauses while gathering his thoughts. "I spoke with a bunch of the guys on the team, and they want to play to honor their injured teammates, by winning this thing. My dilemma is with Teddy and Jack both out, I lose two starting pitchers, and a relief pitcher in Dylan. I know this is short notice and things are still sinking in, but the tournament is coming up Friday. I wanted to ask you, do you have any interest in helping out and pitching on the team for the Enchantment tournament?"

Sarah is standing with her arms folded, leaning against the kitchen wall while listening to Coach Dan's explanation. "Sorry, this is a little confusing for me," replies Sarah. "I recently decided not to pursue anything with the baseball team, and now a few days later, you're asking me if I want to *play* on the team?"

"This is the issue. We have some pitching to get by, but if someone gets hurt or is really getting rocked, you can come in the game and be my insurance policy. Our lower level teams don't have any strong pitchers that I want to use. Hopefully, I won't have to use you. You would be in the dugout being a team player, cheering people on. But if you do want to pitch, I can definitely find a spot to get you out there on the mound. The truth is, you are a really good pitcher. It would only be for the tournament, and it would be helpful to all the guys and me. Will you at least consider playing?" asks Coach Dan.

Sarah takes a moment to think before responding. "Me choosing not to play on the baseball team was for a good reason. But with all that's happened, the team needs help, and you asking, I would be honored to try and do my part and pitch in the tournament," replies Sarah. "Only the tournament, right?" she clarifies.

A smile grows on Coach Dan's face. "That's great news; thank you! Your mom had me check before, and none of the games conflict with the dance or softball games, so that won't be an issue either. This is a tough time for everyone right now, let's just see how it goes."

Sarah looks to her mom seated at the table and observes her with a big wide grin on her face, knowing she may get to see Sarah pitch in a baseball game after all.

"You knew about this and didn't mention it to me?" vocalizes Sarah.

"This whole thing came together in the last half hour. Dan's been on the phone, and I just found out as well," explains Kathrine.

"Well your mom was a little optimistic you would want to play and help out. So, I brought along a uniform that should fit you," Coach Dan says as he takes socks, pants, and a number twenty-seven uniform out of a bag and lays them on the table.

"These things look older than Babe Ruth," says Sarah as she starts rubbing the worn tattered fabric with a look of disgust. "Not enough new uniforms to go around?" she continues sarcastically.

"This uniform has been in my trunk for a while, so like the Babe, it may just smell a little like hot dogs and nachos."

"That's so gross," replies Sarah.

"So, we have three games. I'll email your mom the schedule. Thanks again for playing; it's a huge help to me and the team, and it should be fun!" Dan walks over to Kathrine and gives her a pleasant hug goodbye, and proceeds to head out the door.

Sarah observing, *I may actually be warming up a little to this Mom and Dan thing.*

Kathrine excitedly and supportively says, "Well this will be fun! Pitching baseball seems to have worked out after all. Now you get to play in the tournament." Enjoying the tone and the good feelings, Kathrine attempts to be funny too. "Well, when the games get a little boring, you can always flirt with Stryker on the bench!"

Sarah laughs. "Wow! You're in a good mood Mom; acting all giddy, you must be in love or something, but remember, you're still not funny!" Sarah pauses. "It's all still settling in, but it should be fun. I better start throwing with Shane today. Evan is not going to be happy when he finds out he has to catch for me again. I'm going to text Stryker and tell him I'm playing," she says as she picks up her phone.

"You should text Kayla to let her know that things around the Enchantment Under the Sea dance just got a lot busier," suggests Kathrine.

A light goes off in Sarah's head, "That's right!!!, I have to go back to school to help Kayla. And, I'm going to have way less time to work on the dance with practice for both teams."

Well, her mom was correct. Things just got a lot busier.

Chapter 12
PLAY BALL

▪▪
▪▪

FRANK ALEXANDER STARTED the Enchantment Under the Sea Baseball Tournament in 1997. His first issue as tournament director was the local printer telling him there were too many letters in the title, Enchantment Under the Sea Baseball Tournament, to fit on the T-shirts. Frank worked through that issue and hundreds of other, to get the tournament where it is today.

Frank grew up in Boston, played hockey as a kid, and was exposed to lots of hockey tournaments in the area with his favorite being the Beanpot. The Beanpot is a hockey tournament that started back in the 1950s with four local college teams competing for the Beanpot trophy. The "Beanpot" is a nod to Boston's history with baked beans. The tournament raises thousands of dollars for local charities each year. Frank took that community spirit from Boston and brought it to Redondo Beach. His sons were playing baseball at the time when his neighbor, Mrs. Lana Berz, was working on additional ways to raise money for the community. Frank had the idea and knowledge for the baseball tournament. Lana steered him in the right direction and to the right people. Today it is another fund-raising arm for "Motion in the Ocean" to help keep the beaches and ocean clean.

* * *

Coach Dan calls in the players from their final practice on Thursday before the tournament begins. The focus of the team has been good. They all went together after practice one afternoon earlier in the week to visit their injured teammates at the hospital. It was hard seeing their friends hurting physically like that, but they all learned something from their experience and were honored and excited to play on their behalf.

"Make sure you're all here on time tomorrow! There are going to be four teams so finding practice space beforehand may be a little tight," explains Coach Dan at the end of the talk.

The short week of baseball practice has gone well for Sarah. Coach Nevs from softball was happy to work around Sarah's baseball practice schedule to get her individual softball work done. The first baseball practice Sarah attended, Coach Dan started with a speech, "We need to represent our school with class and character this weekend. The community is watching, and we all need to band together as one to have a successful tournament."

Sarah took that as the "please be nice to Sarah" speech, and she greatly appreciated his support. All the guys have been totally awesome about her playing, and she feels like a real part of the team. Hanging out with Stryker each day at practice had done wonders for advancing their relationship as well.

Sarah has been pleasantly surprised at how excited others have been that she's playing in the baseball tournament as well. The girls on the softball team are all fired up and talked about it throughout the week. Kayla rallied some of the volleyball girls, and they will all go together as a group to support Sarah. She has also had a great response from many of the teachers and classmates who are wishing her good luck. As a good marketing person, Sarah's response is always the same, "Thank you, I may not even get to pitch, but please don't forget to buy your tickets in advance to the Enchantment Under the Sea dance Saturday night!"

Publicity also took a huge upward swing when Krista Stern, the Trout family neighbor and good friend, signed off her Channel 5 nightly news show by reporting,

> *"If you're looking for something fun to do this weekend, the annual Enchantment Under the Sea Baseball Tournament kicks off Friday night in Redondo Beach. This year the tournament will feature its first female player. Sarah Trout, my friend and neighbor, will be playing for South Redondo Beach High school. I'm surprised it took this long! Good luck, Sarah! And that's all for tonight."*

Coach Dan waves Sarah over before she heads into the dugout. "I know I talked about maybe not even needing you to pitch, but there's definitely a buzz around town about you playing now as well. I will do my best to get you in for a few innings."

Sarah smiles and says, "Thank you! I am excited! People I don't even know are saying 'good luck' to me." Sarah's smile grows wider as she continues, "And I got like over a hundred new social media followers just from today!"

"All right let's not get caught up in all the hype and social media, Sarah," chuckles Coach Dan. "You'll pitch great; just stay focused."

Stryker carries his bat bag over his shoulder as he turns to leave, "Hey, Sarah, do you need a ride home? My dad's here."

Sarah appreciates her new teammate's kindness. "I wish I was heading home; I'm going inside to help Kayla finish things up for the dance."

"I'm sorry again I couldn't help more with the dance. We have people coming into town tonight to stay with us for the weekend. My mom always has lots of plans. We're going to some play Saturday night, so the dance is definitely out for me," explains Stryker.

Sarah is disappointed upon hearing that Stryker will not be at the dance and quickly senses that this is the girl who talked about Stryker as "my boy" on social media. Sarah coyly asks, "You have family coming into town to stay with you?"

"No, they're not family. My mom's best friend from college is coming. We've vacationed in Mammoth with them growing up and usually spend holidays together. They've got some kids our age, it's usually fun," replies Stryker. He sees his dad waiting in the car while Sarah seems to be lost in her thoughts. Stryker turns to Sarah again and says playfully, "Well I'll see you tomorrow! Your first baseball game, the big lobster tournament, should be fun."

Sarah leans into Stryker and gives him a hug goodbye. "Who doesn't love lobster?" she playfully responds. "Thanks for all your help with the guys; they've all been really great about me playing, I know you've watched out for me."

Stryker says proudly, "Hey I mean you gotta keep your pitcher happy," as he releases from their hug and heads to his dad's waiting car.

Sarah makes a direct beeline to the science department, opens the door, and is surprised to find only a few people in there working. There are boxes lined up in a very organized fashion against the back wall with Kayla sitting there working on her laptop.

Kayla looks up to see Sarah enter the room. "What's up, Miss Baseball. Are you ready to go?"

Sarah glances around the room and sees how well put together all the dance stuff looks. She's a little surprised. "Kayla, you have everything ready to go; you've done so great! I'm so sorry I haven't been here to help," Sarah says as she pulls up a chair and sits.

"I know you've been super busy. Mrs. Berz came in early this morning, and we got through everything. We saved so much time since she knows all the pieces and where they've been placed in the past. It was fun; don't worry about it. She can be pretty entertaining anyways, and only two days to go," says Kayla.

"Well it looks great! I've been so busy dealing with all the baseball stuff that time just flew by. I can't believe the dance is only in two days! What did Mrs. Berz think of the mermaid?" Sarah excitedly asks.

Kayla, with a big grin on her face, says, "She *loved* it!" She once again puts her finger to her lips, making the "quiet, don't tell anybody" sign.

Sarah realizes that there is not much she can do now until dance setup begins on Saturday. "We have games tomorrow and early Saturday, so hopefully I will be here early in the afternoon; I'm so fired up."

"Sounds good! By the way, how are things going being around Stryker all the time at baseball?" inquires Kayla.

"I don't know anymore. He has this mystery girl visiting this weekend he says is a family friend, but then he said he can't make the dance. I mean, we hug after practices, so I guess that counts as something."

Kayla sarcastically responds, "Yes, wow, hugging is good! You've come such a long way from handshaking, you're practically married." Kayla laughs at her own joke as Sarah rolls her eyes. "Well you and I will have a blast at the dance," says Kayla. "The band Mrs. Berz got is super good. Just for this dance, they call themselves Marvin Berry and the Starlighters, which is the name of the dance band from the movie *Back to the Future*. They're normally a country band called Tail Gates Down. Mrs. Berz says she pays them well. This is their fifth time playing the dance. She even had them learn the songs from the Enchantment Under the Sea dance scene in the movie to make it authentic. She played me some of their music this morning and it was good. You know, *real* oldies and some fun dance music, stuff like that. It'll be a good time."

"That's great. I think I've heard them play before," replies Sarah.

Kayla glances at her phone and starts texting before saying, "Just so you know, I'll be there for the first game tomorrow with all the girls, and we'll be cheering for you, so hopefully you'll get to pitch. But either way we'll still be shouting and embarrassing you! Text me if anything changes."

Both girls stand up and give each other a hug as Sarah heads out the door home. This is all really happening.

* * *

The drive to the tournament was fun and filled with anticipation. Andrew came along for the ride and was acting silly in the back. He brought his plastic Wiffle ball bat in the car and kept hitting himself in the head, saying, "Home run, home run, home run," as Sarah and Kathrine laughed loudly, which just made Andrew do it more.

"Are you excited to play? Nervous?" Kathrine inquires.

"Definitely a little nervous, but I'm excited just to get out there and pitch. Coach Dan said most players haven't batted against a knuckleball pitcher before, so if I can throw strikes or make them think they're strikes, then I should be fine."

As they approach the parking lot for the high school, it is obvious that there is something festive going on.

Frank Alexander and his merry band of volunteers have been very busy. There are large groups of red and white balloons tied to the fence at the entrance. A little farther down the road is a large Enchantment Under the Sea sign against a wall of light blue crepe paper made to look like waves against the backstop wall. Every year, the most popular volunteer role is getting to dress up in the 'Sammy the Shark' outfit and roam around the facility. The blue and white costume, which can get a little warm, clearly draws the most attention. Sammy the Shark walks the sidewalk at the main entrance, baseball bat in hand, waving to cars, trying to bring in customers. And of course, there are lots of pictures with little kids, some not too eager, but Sammy is the face of the tournament.

Kathrine pulls into the lot, a little surprised to see two TV news vans, for Channel Five and Channel Nine, parked on the grass. There is a lot of activity everywhere. People are raking and lining the field, stocking the snack bar, lining trash cans, and teams are warming up.

"Do they always have TV trucks here?" Sarah wonders aloud.

"I don't know, but there's definitely excitement in the air," replies Kathrine as they approach Coach Dan sitting with a few of the players.

"If I knew having a girl play on the team was going to bring out all the TV stations, I would have done it years ago," Coach Dan comments as everyone laughs. "Every year we get a TV van out here. They go interview Sammy the Shark and do some wacky bit with him, but *two* TV vans here on a Friday--this is a first."

Kathrine's phone buzzes. She looks at it. "I think Krista had a hand in this. Listen to this." Kathrine reads the text aloud. "The other station heard me promoting the event, so they just jumped in. As far as the tournament goes, any publicity is good publicity, right?" Krista also texted Kathrine asking how "Danny boy" was doing, with a happy face and lipstick kiss emoji, but Kathrine did not mention those remarks to the others.

Coach Dan takes the next hour to run the team through drills to get ready for the start of the game. South Redondo Beach opens the tournament against Penn High School. Penn has been a good baseball program throughout the years, but with only a few returning starters, this season probably will not be one of their best.

The crowd settles in with some standing room only against the outfield fence. All the publicity from the local news, plus word of mouth about Sarah playing baseball, has really brought out the Redondo Beach local fans; Sarah's family and friends among them.

To kick the game off, a fully uniformed local T-ball team being corralled by their coaches stands on the pitcher's mound and shouts in unison, "Play Ball" as the T-ballers all throw the opening pitch to a parent standing near home plate. South Redondo Beach versus Penn is underway.

The game begins with Redondo taking an early 3-0 lead into the third inning on a key ground rule double by Stryker with the bases loaded. That lead increases to 7-0 in the sixth as Evan connects with a hanging curve ball for a grand slam, his first homer of the year. Sean, who is Redondo's best pitcher, has been throwing strikes and is pitching well. The mood in the dugout is very upbeat.

"Nice home run, Evan; could you jog around the bases any slower?" teases Coach Dan.

"It was my first one, Coach! I wanted to make it last for all my fans!" Evan excitedly responds.

Sarah sits on the bench next to Stryker, laughing. "You really crushed that."

"Well don't celebrate too much, Evan; you need to go warm up Sarah," says Coach Dan.

Sarah hears her name called and immediately stands up and grabs her glove. Evan, who is so happy about his home run, doesn't even complain that someone else could be warming up Sarah. Evan grabs his glove and catcher's gear to get ready.

Stryker looks up to Sarah smiling, "Good luck, surfer girl."

Sarah and Evan jog down to the bullpen to warm up. The crowd sees Sarah and starts cheering loudly. A smile comes to Sarah's face as she gives a wave to Andrew, who is jumping up and down frantically and waving. Many of the fans are standing and getting ready to record Sarah's pitching on their phones.

"Let's go, Sarah; show them what you got!" Kayla yells.

Sarah's warm-up throws with Evan go well. Considering how nervous she is, throwing the first three pitches past Evan in the dirt wasn't that big of a deal.

The inning ends, and Coach Dan signals for Sarah to come in from the bullpen and pitch. Coach Dan walks out to the mound to meet Sarah and hands her the ball.

"Just do your thing, kid," says Coach Dan as he glances toward Kathrine in the stands before heading back to the dugout.

Evan says, "You got this," as he goes behind the plate.

Sarah has gotten most of her nerves out during her bullpen session. She is feeling confident and ready to go. The first batter for Penn steps into the batter's box. Sarah looks in at the batter. She takes a deep breath. *Remember to throw overhand* she jokes to herself. The batter swings at the first pitch, popping up the ball to third for an easy out. Sarah thought her knuckleball was a little flat but was happy with the late movement and also with the first out. The crowd, led by Kayla and the softball girls, cheers loudly.

The rest of the game goes well for Sarah and the South Redondo Beach baseball team. She faces eight more batters—a couple of walks, a couple of strikeouts, and a good defensive play by Stryker that all contributed to South Redondo Beach winning with a score of 7-0. The teams go through the ceremonial handshake at home plate. "Good game, good game, good game, good game, you suck, good game, good game, good game, good game, good game, good game, good game, good game, good game, good game."

Sarah receives lots of attention from family and friends after the game as she completes a short interview with the school newspaper.

Kathrine chimes in, "Great job, sweetie," as Andrew runs over to hug her.

"The team awarded me the game ball! I'm so excited; I can't believe I pitched, and we won!!" Sarah replies smiling. As Kathrine leans in and hugs Sarah, her daughter continues to ramble, "Once I got through a couple of batters, it didn't even seem like that big of a deal; wait, that came out wrong. I mean, I felt like pitching was just what I was supposed to be doing."

"I'm proud of you; Grandpa would be very proud of you," says Kathrine.

"Thank you. I felt like he was here helping," replies Sarah.

Coach Dan comes over to hug Kathrine and give Andrew a little pat on his head. "Sarah did great! I would use her again if needed. We play two games tomorrow morning, and hopefully the finals are one of them."

Shane comes by with a few of his buddies and checks in with his sister. "I guess me practicing with you all these years has finally paid off, huh," he snickers as he hugs his sister.

"You mean practicing all these *weeks*," says Sarah.

Kayla and the volleyball girls, as well as the softball girls, come to congratulate Sarah too. Some young girls ask Sarah for her autograph, which makes her very embarrassed but secretly happy as well. She signs their tournament programs and takes selfies with them. The crowd slowly disperses for the evening as Kathrine, Sarah, and Andrew head to the car as people honk and wave to them as they drive away.

"That was quite the night, young lady," Kathrine says as they arrive home and both drop their bags on the coffee table and flop on the couch in total relaxation mode. Sarah is still in her dirty uniform and is about to go shower, but she is interrupted by her Mom. Kathrine slowly goes through her handbag, looking intently, and pulls out an envelope. She looks directly at Sarah and says, "I have something for you."

Sarah sees the envelope and turns her attention to her mother. "I hope it's free Chipotle coupons."

"No, it's something better than food," as she pauses for a moment and takes a serious tone. "It's actually a letter from your grandfather," Kathrine replies.

Sarah looks confused as she takes the envelope, reading in large capital letters her name "SARAH" written in her grandfather's handwriting, next to a drawing of a 3-D staircase he would always sketch for her. Sarah opens the letter cautiously, not knowing what to expect.

Dear Sarah,

If you're reading this letter that means I'm no longer around. It really was just time for me to go, but it also means that you finally decided to accept your tremendous potential and pitched in a baseball game, and I couldn't be prouder.
Baseball has been in our family for a few generations, I'm glad you got to be part of it. I had written this for you knowing, or should I say "hoping," you would pitch in a baseball game one day. Baseball can provide you with a lifetime of experiences and friendships. I just know that you had that knuckleball moving and shaking today, and hopefully you had a good catcher. I'm very proud of the person you're becoming. Please give a big hug to everyone for me. I love you all.

Love, Grandpa

P.S. keep an eye on that Andrew—he's a wild one.

Sarah holds the letter on her lap and stares into the distance as tears slowly roll down her cheeks.

"Are you OK?" asks Kathrine as she holds her close.

"Yeah, yeah, sorry, just taking this all in. That made me so happy," sighs Sarah as she pauses before handing the letter and envelope back to her mother, who then begins to quickly read through it herself. "After Grandpa's funeral, Coach Dan had mentioned a story Grandpa told him about getting a letter from his grandfather about baseball, but I didn't think anything of it," explains Sarah.

"Your grandfather really loved you. As things started to get worse, he handed me this letter and asked me to give it to you in case you ever pitched in a baseball game. At the time, I didn't think anything of it because playing baseball wasn't even on your radar. Your grandpa must have known, or at least had an idea, that when he passed away, you would try to do something to honor him and play."

Sarah sits there a little stunned, but also elated and emotionally replies with some tears still rolling down her cheeks, "Boy, did Grandpa get that one right!"

Chapter 13
OUT OF LEFT FIELD

▪▪
▪▪

THE EARLY MORNING Saturday game of the Enchantment Under the Sea tournament could not have gone any better for the South Redondo Beach baseball team. Playing against Hermosa Beach High School, the exciting game ended with South Redondo Beach winning 2-1. Oscar, who had been having shoulder tightness for the past few weeks, went out and pitched a complete game. Evan hit his second home run of the year and the defense made no errors to support the victory. Sarah and her teammates were very animated cheering their team on from the bench.

South Redondo Beach successfully moves on to the tournament championship game versus East Torrance High School. As Coach Dan addresses the team before the start of the championship game, he sees Dylan being pushed in a wheelchair by his dad toward the field. With black and blue bruises still covering the right side of his face and both his legs in braces, Dylan gives a wave. Coach Dan enthusiastically points toward Dylan and waves. "Look who's here for the game!"

The team immediately jogs out of the dugout to greet Dylan. He is still in a lot of pain but has a smile on his face. The team exchanges gentle "low fives" with him. "The doctor said I need to get out of the hospital and get some fresh air, so I figured this is the perfect place. The other guys wished they could be here too, but they're here supporting in spirit; I'll be texting them updates," says Dylan.

"I'm really glad you're here Dylan," says Sarah as she pats him gently on his back.

"Sarah Trout playing in the championship game. I wouldn't miss it," replies Dylan still smiling.

Dylan and his parents find a spot along the first-base-line fence to watch. Coach Dan finishes his final pep talk to the team as they wait for the umpires to get the game started and for the booth to announce the starting lineups.

"Wow, it's so great seeing Dylan, but he still looks like he's in a lot of pain," Sarah comments to Coach Dan.

"Dylan and the others still have a long way to go physically and emotionally before they're back to normal again, but some of them seem to be improving," responds Coach Dan as he pauses and quickly changes to championship game mode. "All right Sarah, you pitched great yesterday, but there's a good chance I won't need you to come in and pitch today. Sean's been pitching really well, so this means your baseball career could be coming to a close."

Dan and Kathrine had a previous discussion about how this does not have to be Sarah's last baseball game. Dan would be happy to have her play the whole season, if interested. He was just feeling things out.

"Whatever you need me to do coach. I'm really glad I got to pitch! Got a *boatload* of new followers across social media, but I've got softball games with the girls next week. So, I'm good to go," Sarah replies.

"Boatload? Really? That's what you kids are saying these days, *boatload?*" Coach Dan raises an eyebrow.

Stryker, stretching near the on-deck circle walks over to Sarah with a strained look on his face. "Hey, I don't know if this is going to weird you out or anything, but you should know that Joey Smoak is here, and he's playing for East Torrance."

Sarah looks across the field to see Joey warming up with his teammates. She is a little shaken and surprised. "Wait, what? I thought he moved to Carson?"

"I thought so too, but he's been having some problems with his foster parents. Evan said he heard he was living at his brother's in Torrance. He wasn't here for the other games, so maybe he was out sick or something," says Stryker.

Sarah mumbles to no one in particular, "Or maybe he was in jail."

East Torrance is practicing on one of the backfields. Word has spread quickly in the dugout that Joey is playing for East. Sean had gotten to be a good friend of Joey's while he was at South Redondo and gives Joey a yell from across the field with a clenched fist and his arm raised over his head. "Joey!"

Joey hears the loud yell and gives a casual acknowledgment wave back.

Coach Dan walks over to check in on Sarah, "Are you good?"

Sarah puts on a brave face but is clearly rattled. "I'm fine; he's the one with the problem."

The game again falls into place nicely for South Redondo Beach. Sean looks good pitching from the first inning by striking out the East Torrance first three batters. Stryker and Oscar both hit doubles with the bases loaded. East Torrance makes some costly errors in the field and, heading into the sixth inning, Redondo is up 10-2.

Coach Dan comes over to Sarah with a smile on his face. "Sean has just about reached his pitch limit, and Oscar jammed his knee sliding into second on his double, so he can't pitch. Do you have a few more innings in you?"

Sarah reacts a little surprised that she is needed. She thought Oscar was going to pitch after Sean but had not noticed him sitting against the dugout fence with a large ice pack on his knee.

Sarah jumps up and grabs her glove. Sounding a little panicked, "I need to warm up, let's go!"

"Relax, relax, that's what you're going to do now," says Coach Dan feeling her stress.

Sarah hustles down to the bullpen to warm up with Trevor, who has never caught for her before. South Redondo Beach batters swing at some early pitches and make three quick outs to end the inning. Coach Dan waves to Sarah from the dugout to come in and pitch as Evan heads to the mound to meet her.

Sarah sounds concerned and quickly says, "I didn't warm up enough; Trevor had to keep chasing the ball."

Evan, beaming with confidence after a very successful weekend hitting, says, "You'll be fine; we're killing them anyway."

Sarah gets in her final warm-up pitches to Evan; some of them a bit erratic with Evan doing his best to block them. The mood of the championship game is pretty quiet. With all the excitement from the tournament's opening games passed, the media coverage has moved on to the next news cycle. With the score still 10-2 in Redondo's favor, things have remained pretty calm. Until now. Sarah does not get off to the best start and walks the first batter she faces on four straight balls.

Coach Dan offers encouragement from the dugout, "Just settle down; settle down, Sarah. You're fine."

The East Torrance team senses a possible opportunity to get back in the game. Sarah waits for the next batter, trying to calm herself down. *I got this; I got this.* The next batter steps into the box.

Sarah gets ready to throw her pitch, when a player yells very loudly and aggressively from the East dugout, "This chick's got nothing! I think she's wearing a wig! She's a mess! She can't pitch!"

Sarah is stunned by the loud, aggressive outburst that breaks the silence of the game and turns to see Joey Smoak yelling from the dugout fence.

All the fans and players turn their attention to Joey, who continues yelling aggressively, "This chick can't pitch; she's no good!" Joey continues yelling while pointing at Sarah now with his finger. "That's right, I'm talking about you, two-seven!"

There is an awkward silence from the uncomfortable crowd. Kathrine, who is grading some quiz papers while watching from the stands, listens to the outburst. She knows who Joey is from school but had never seen him like this. Kathrine stands up and starts stepping down from the bleachers, looking around, and mumbles to no one in particular, "Is somebody going to shut that kid up?"

Trying to rattle an opposing player is not against the rules by any means, but Joey's aggressive tone sounds more personal than for the love of the game.

Sarah is visibly shaken by Joey's verbal attacks and tries to calm herself down by stepping off the rubber. She has seen enough of Joey to know that anything is possible, and this would not be the first time he charged the mound to get her. Sarah throws her next pitch into the dirt for ball one. Joey starts yelling again as his teammates join him, sensing Sarah is flustered. She throws the next three pitches into the dirt for balls two, three and four. The yelling from the East Torrance bench intensifies.

Coach Dan calls the umpire for a time-out and heads out to the mound to talk to Sarah emphatically. "Don't let Joey's crap bother you! Like you said, he's the one with the problem; just settle down and throw your pitch!" As Coach Dan returns to the dugout, he heads over to talk to the home-plate umpire.

After a quick discussion, the umpire calls the East Torrance manager out to home plate with Coach Dan. The umpire tells them, "Cheering for your team is one thing, but you have to control that kid. He can't be screaming and yelling like that."

The East coach looks over toward his team bench before calmly saying to Dan, "Joey just started with us this week; that's all I've been around him. You probably know him a lot better than I do. Does he normally act like this?"

"I was told Joey's having some problems at home," Coach Dan sympathetically replies.

The East coach responds, "I was about to say something to him about all the yelling before you called me over, so I'm good telling him to knock it off."

The coaches walk back to their respective teams as the East Torrance coach pulls Joey over to the side and has a quick discussion. Joey looking upset, knocks over some bats before heading to the end of the bench to sit alone. The East Torrance team and their fans start to cheer loudly again, encouraging their team to continue this comeback.

Sarah, still a little rattled, hits the next batter to load the bases. Evan, who is struggling a bit chasing down Sarah's wild pitches, calls for Sarah to throw her first fastball to the East Torrance cleanup hitter. Sarah's mediocre fastball is right down the middle and gets crushed for a grand slam and brings the score of the game to 10-6.

The East Torrance bench and fans are cheering wildly now as the last run crosses home plate. Joey, who looks like he is out of his momentary funk from his coach's scolding, is cheering again as well.

Coach Dan is pacing back and forth in the dugout, trying to determine if he has anyone else to pitch if Sarah cannot finish.

Evan comes out from behind the plate for a brief mound visit. Evan tells Sarah, "No more fastballs."

Sarah again tries to settle herself down. She catches a break when the next East Torrance batter checks his swing early in the count and hits a weak a ground ball to first base for the first out of the inning. Sarah feels a little relieved and throws a sharp knuckleball to the next batter, who pops up for the second out. Her fortunate little streak ends quickly as she throws a flat knuckleball that the next East Torrance batter homers to centerfield.

As the batter is rounding the bases, Stryker comes over to the mound to offer encouragement to Sarah but pauses for a second as he sees a teardrop fall from her eye. Stryker feels horrible for the girl he really likes, gets a rush of emotion and just wants to give her a big hug but backs off from doing that in the middle of the championship game and just pats her on her back with his glove. "Come on, you got this."

Sarah retires the next batter quickly as the inning ends. She jogs back to the dugout and is met by Coach Dan. "Are you OK? It's the last inning. I can get Trevor warming up if you can't finish."

Sarah still shaken up and sniffling back some tears, says, "I want to finish the game." She sits down at the end of the bench, trying to collect her thoughts and settle herself down. Stryker comes over from the adjoining bench and sits next to her and she doesn't even notice. Sarah knows what a mess she's made of this game.

Suddenly, Sarah feels a soft warm hand grab her hand from the side and momentarily holds it. Sarah, a little confused, turns to see Stryker sitting across the bench from her, holding her hand gently. Their eyes lock for a brief second as a smile comes to both of their faces.

The precious moment quickly comes to an end as Coach Dan yells, "Stryker, you're on deck; grab a bat. Let's go!"

Stryker releases Sarah's hand as he jumps up to find his bat. Sarah looks around the dugout to see if anyone saw their "moment" and thinks to herself, *that was the sweetest thing anyone has ever done.*

South Redondo Beach goes down quietly and quickly in their half of the inning. Sarah walks out to the mound, feeling much more relaxed and secure now, and makes quick work of East Torrance in their final at bats. After a first pitch ground out and a looping pop fly to right field, Sarah feels in complete control as the Redondo crowd begins roaring in preparation for the final out. Sarah glances toward the East Torrance bench and sees Joey Smoak swinging a bat, getting loose in the on-deck circle.

With the current batter's count two and two, Sarah knows, *I need to get this last out.* Sarah winds up and throws a sharp knuckleball that sinks right as the batter swings left and misses for strike three, and the South Redondo Beach crowd erupts in cheers!

The team rushes toward the pitcher's mound to celebrate their championship win and congratulate Sarah as Dylan excitedly videos on his phone from the side. As the celebrating diminishes, East Torrance is waiting for South Redondo Beach at home plate for handshakes. "Good game, good game, good game, good game, good game, good game, good game, loser, good game, good game, good game, good game, good game, good game, good game."

Sarah gets through the line and realizes that Joey is not in it. She glances to the East Torrance dugout area and sees no signs of Joey. Maybe it is better this way.

Sarah and the rest of the team collect their stuff and head into the stands. Kathrine greets her with a big hug. "Great job, Sarah. Another Enchantment Under the Sea championship for South Redondo Beach."

Sarah is very relieved the game is over and just sighs, "Thank you." She gives a wave goodbye to a smiling Dylan and his parents as they wheel him to their car.

Stryker comes over to the group to say hello to Kathrine and turns to Sarah. "Hey, congrats again! My dad's here, and we've got a lot going on, but have fun tonight at the dance. I'm sure it will be *enchanting*," he says as Sarah laughs and gives him a long hug goodbye.

"I wish you were coming tonight," Sarah says.

Kathrine, who is listening, turns her back away from both of them to give them a bit of privacy.

Stryker replies, "Yeah, I do too; I'm sure it will be great, I'll text you later." He continues smiling at Sarah as he heads off.

Coach Dan comes over to Kathrine grinning and says, "Your little girl did pretty well out there."

Kathrine smiles back at Dan as Sarah interrupts, "I was terrible. I couldn't even throw strikes. I'm just glad we won."

Kathrine's body language changes after Sarah's comments, as she turns to Dan, "What was Joey's problem? I was getting worried for Sarah at one point; he seemed a bit out of control."

"I don't know what that was all about; his coach didn't know either. At this point it's probably better that Joey doesn't go to South Redondo anymore or see Sarah."

Kathrine has never heard Dan seem concerned about Joey's actions before. "Do you think Sarah has anything to worry about? Joey just better stay away from her," conveys Kathrine as Sarah is half listening to their conversation while talking with some of the softball girls.

"I think she's fine; Joey has just had a rough go of it lately," he explains. Coach Dan turns to Sarah changing the subject and says, "You can keep the uniform as a keepsake for your baseball career if you'd like. You earned it.... unless you think you want to keep wearing it?"

Sarah replies sarcastically, "Ha ha...I will not be needing this uniform. Mom would just sell it in a garage sale anyway. I'm very happy to have the Enchantment championship as my last baseball game. End on a high note."

Frank Alexander, who is closing down the event with other volunteers, calls over Coach Dan to give him his box of winning-player trophies and the "Poseidon." The "Poseidon" is the 5-foot-high winning-team trophy made in the likeness of the Greek god "Poseidon" for the Enchantment Under the Sea theme. The winning team keeps the trophy until the next year and gets the school name and year engraved on the side. Frank hands everything over and says, "I'm sorry I couldn't get them to you sooner. I know some kids have already left. We stopped doing a ceremony a few years back; coaches decided people just want to get going, but congrats again. Awesome tournament!"

"Not a problem, Frank; you guys do a great job with this whole event," says Coach Dan.

Frank puts his arm around Dan's shoulder and steers him away from the other workers. "First, please tell Kathrine I was so sorry to hear about her dad. We've been so busy; I didn't get a chance to tell her."

"Of course, of course," says Dan.

"The other thing was, I saw what went on with Smoak today," continues Frank. "Just so you know, I heard he had some altercation with some girl in El Segundo two nights ago. I don't know the whole story, but I thought I would mention it to you."

Coach Dan thanks Frank for his update. "I'll try to look into it."

Most everyone is gone as Sarah and Kathrine say their final goodbyes and get into their car in the mostly empty parking lot.

"I heard them making announcements during the game promoting the dance," says Sarah.

"I heard them as well. I also heard Shane is giving you guys a hand today; that's nice of your brother," says Kathrine. Sarah, looking at her phone, is only half listening to her mom. Kathrine comments, hoping to get her attention, "And I see that's not the only *hand* you were offered today."

Sarah stops looking at her phone, and her eyes open wide as she quickly picks up her head, and animatedly exclaims, "You saw that! You saw Stryker hold my hand. I thought no one saw it; nobody said anything! It was only for a second. Oh my God, that's so embarrassing!"

"I'm your mother. I see everything. And yes, I saw him hold your hand. With Joey screaming like a maniac and the home runs you gave up, I knew you were hurting; Stryker's stock has gone way up with me," explains Kathrine.

Sarah glances out the window lost in thought, and says mockingly, "Just so you know, you're still not funny," as she grins at her mother. "And believe me, Stryker's stock has gone way up with me as well."

Chapter 14

LET'S DANCE

KATHRINE IS HAPPY to drive the girls to the high school early. The Enchantment Under the Sea dance is hours away, and she knows how excited the girls are about putting it together. The mood in the car now is much lighter than the Joey Smoak tenseness earlier in the day. Sarah and Kayla are looking at their decoration's layout together.

"I think we're good to go as long as people show up to help set up," says Kayla.

Kathrine injects some optimism. "It will all work out, girls; the dance will go well, and you'll both have a great night." The girls both look at each other and smile in agreement.

"Sarah and I have a 'no phones pact' during the dance so we don't miss anything," says Kayla.

"Turning off your phone anytime is always a good idea," replies Kathrine.

Sarah folds up their plans and stuffs them into her backpack along with the clothes she is changing into for the dance.

"Now mom, I know you and Coach Dan are both chaperoning the dance. Please do not do anything weird to embarrass me. I'm probably the only kid at the dance whose mother is there, and to make it worse, she's there with her new boyfriend!"

Kayla, laughing at Sarah, asks, "Coach Dan is working the dance too? How cute, and from Sarah's comment, I guess you guys are official now."

"Yes, Dan and I are working the dance, like a little date. And if 'official' means happy in our relationship, then yes, we're official," says Kathrine.

"If I see you guys slow dancing or twerking, I think I'll throw up," says Sarah grimacing.

"Well, since you're working the dance, you'll be the one cleaning up that puke," says Kathrine laughing as she pulls her blue Honda CRV up to the outside door of the cafeteria.

An empty police car is already parked near the dance entrance. The girls say their goodbyes to Sarah's mom as they enthusiastically jump out of the car and head into the dance. There is already a group of committee members unloading folding tables and putting folding chairs up against the wall. A few students are cutting open bags of pretzels and putting them into bowls. The band Marvin Berry and the Starlighters is in there as well. Marvin struggles with a broken wheel on a dolly as they get the last of their amps to the stage.

Mrs. Berz sees the girls walk in and heads over to greet them. "Hello ladies," she says with her arms extended out wide, "and welcome to the Enchantment Under the Sea dance." She gives the girls fist bumps. "All of these boxes here are your stuff; that ladder is for you. Just look at these cafeteria walls and ceiling as a blank canvas; now you just need to get creative."

Sarah and Kayla both look at each other smiling and say excitedly, "Let's do this!"

For many years the dance was located in the school gym, but one year it conflicted with a big volleyball tournament on campus, so the dance had to be moved to the cafeteria. Mrs. Berz ended up liking the cafeteria layout much better than the gym, so she never moved the dance back.

The girls are very motivated and get through some boxes quickly. The octopus and smiling clam look a little out of place on the wall by themselves, but there is plenty more to come. Kayla, who is standing on the top step of the ladder, slips and catches herself before falling off. The girls share a nervous laugh for a moment, discussing what they would have to do if one of them fell off the ladder and got hurt.

The girls get through a couple more boxes as Sarah checks the time and sees it is almost three o'clock; four hours till the dance. Kayla carries over a new box as the girls pull out some dolphin and gray whale decorations. Sarah, holding them up to the wall to see how they will look, hears someone call her name. She turns around and is a little surprised to see Shane and three friends arrive already, but she is happy they remembered the other ladder.

Shane says proudly, "Here we are, four people at three o'clock, just like you said, ready to work and on time."

Sarah shakes her head, laughing. "I'm glad you're here, but I *said* three people at four o'clock," she explains once again as Kayla stops going through the box and laughs with Sarah. "Mom always says you're not very good at listening, but in this case I'm happy about it."

"Mom never says I don't listen. I know she says Andrew doesn't listen."

Sarah being more emphatic, says, "Of course you don't think she says you don't listen, and why? Because you *don't* listen!"

Shane shakes his head for a second, a bit confused, but moves on to introduce his friends. "This is Nico and Matthew, and you've both met Harry before." Everybody does the "nod hello" thing as they take a look around at all the activity going on.

Harry comments to Nico, "There are some fine-looking ladies setting up this dance."

Sarah walks over to the boxes numbered nine, ten, and eleven and points to them. "Shane, these boxes are yours. Please be careful up on the ladder; Kayla almost fell before. Just tape the streamers hanging from the ceiling like we discussed, then we can attach the paper fish on the bottom."

Shane, acting cocky in front of his friends, "I've done this setup a lot more than you; I know what to do." Sarah thanks her brother again for helping out, and he responds with, "Mom told me about all the drama with Smoak at the game today. Screw that guy!" And playfully continues, "If you need your big brother to take care of you, I've been known to kick some ass."

"I don't need protecting. I can handle my own stuff, and by the way, you've never even been in a fight, so thanks Mr. UFC, but no thanks," Sarah says.

Sarah turns to go back through the next box with Kayla; they pull out some small plastic statues of Poseidon holding a trident that match a larger statue that will be placed near the dance entrance. The girls are determining if they have enough of each display to fit on all the tables.

Kayla raises her head and turns to Sarah. "Holy crap, look at your brother."

Sarah looks up to see Shane and his friends all laughing as they've all taken off their shirts to work. Sarah gets up and walks over to her brother, a bit annoyed. "Seriously? You guys need your shirts off?"

"I remember getting a little sweaty working last year," says Shane as the boys keep laughing.

"The cafeteria is air-conditioned; it's actually cold in here," says Sarah as the boy's start stretching their arms as if they were about to begin working out and continue laughing. "You guys are so lame. I know you're just trying to show off for all the girls working in here."

Harry starts posing and flexing his muscles while pointing, "I think the beach is that way."

"Just relax; we're just having a little fun. I guess they say you get what you pay for," says Shane as he opens the boxes and starts pulling out rolls of streamers and goes back to work.

Sarah heads back to Kayla and their boxes. Kayla says, "The timing may not be right for this, but your brother really does have a nice body, just saying."

"Surfing everyday will do that for you. I'm just really glad they're helping out," says a calmer Sarah. "My concern is if they start taking their pants off, now that's when we'll have a real problem." Sarah continues playfully.

* * *

The Lomita neighborhood isn't the greatest. The gate to enter the apartment complex is hanging on by its last screw. The apartment is small and run down and has Papa John's pizza boxes thrown carelessly in the corner. Joey Smoak puts the case of Budweiser into the refrigerator, opening one up for himself and chugging most of it down. Joey's buddies Lou and Jaime are sitting on the mostly torn couch.

"Bring some of those beers in here, bro," shouts Jaime as Joey grabs three more beers in one hand while finishing his beer with the other. "It's cool your brother's letting you crash here," says Jaime.

"Trust me, it's not that cool when your brother shows up whacked out of his mind and terrorizes you. My brother's insane. It makes me miss living with the Martins already. The sooner I can get some cash and get out of here, the better," Joey declares.

"I stole some whiskey from my old man, so drink up, boys," says Lou, holding out a silver flask of Jack Daniels for anyone interested.

Joey grabs the flask and takes a good swig, making a face from the harsh taste. "Woo, that shit is strong," says Joey as he composes himself for a second. "So, let's talk about getting paid tonight. When I worked the Redondo baseball camp last summer, I had a master key that I used to get into the school when pain in the ass kids needed to go to the bathroom or see the trainer. When camp ended,

I told them one of the other coaches had the key, but I still have it. I know the key still works because one-night last month I snuck into the high school and used it. Took some shit and got out. The dance tonight should be packed, and tickets are like fifteen bucks. Last year, I hung outside and watched their whole ticket operation. I say we go check it out. Once we can figure out where they move the money to, we can use my key to get in that office, take the money, and be long gone before anyone even knows it's missing."

Lou and Jaime both take long drinks from their beers. Lou says, "Well that seems a simple enough plan. Doesn't hurt to go take a look around. I'm in."

Jaime, who is carefully peeling the label off his beer bottle, quickly chimes in, "I'm in too."

Lou adds, "And if we run into any trouble, I will handle it. He flicks open his switchblade knife and stabs it hard into an empty box on the table.

"Just try not to stab yourself," laughs Jaime unimpressed.

Joey holds his bottle up high as he's ready to make a toast. "All I know boys, is we're gonna get into some trouble tonight," he says as the others raise their bottles and clank them together in unison. Joey says in an angry tone, "Payback is a bitch!"

* * *

The rest of the dance setup goes extremely well for the girls. Kayla and Sarah have piled all the empty numbered boxes along with other unused dance items in a hallway closet. Mrs. Berz has been in and out of the building most of the afternoon.

"Girls, the place looks fabulous. I'm so impressed with both of you." Sarah and Kayla smile proudly at each other. "All of the walls look fantastic; the ceiling over the dance floor has never looked so full. I saw Shane and his guys were working hard. I didn't want to slow them down by asking about the shirtless look," chuckles Mrs. Berz.

"Shane and those guys did so great. I don't even care anymore about their lack of shirts either," says Sarah.

Mrs. Berz asks the girls to walk with her so she can show them the entire event operation. With an hour to go before the doors open, there is still some fine tuning to be done, plus "the mermaid." There are lots of students starting to hang around outside the entrance. Mrs. Berz did anticipate a good crowd with all the Sarah baseball publicity, but even this has exceeded her expectations.

"I had them move the ticket-selling tables outside so we can start selling early. They've been selling for a while now and we still have long lines."

"Where do they put all their money?" asks Kayla.

Mrs. Berz is listening but surveying some students trying to close an entrance door. "They have cash boxes to put their money in. We don't take credit cards. When the cash boxes get full, Vice Principal Ardito moves the money to her office. We have a security guard posted at the table at all times for the ticket seller's safety as well," continues Mrs. Berz. She walks behind the sellers and points to the money boxes. "During a busy dance like tonight, we can take in over $3,000 in cash. After we pay for expenses, the rest of the money gets donated to "Motion in the Ocean."

Mrs. Berz leads the girls back inside and walks them to the arched entrance way, which gives you the illusion that you are walking through a giant whale's open mouth. The area around it has been decorated with daisies, irises, lilies, and carnations of all colors. The archway leads you to twenty-five round tables with various *Finding Nemo* and *Shark Tales* tablecloths with ocean decorations on them. If you didn't know any better the room could easily pass as a wedding reception for Aquaman.

Mrs. Berz shows the girls the location where "the mermaid" will be located, which is next to the fruit-punch and cheese-and-cracker table. She points to the far wall near the stage which has the movie *Back to the Future* projected on it. The movie will run on the wall for the entire dance. Mrs. Berz walks to the band and introduces Sarah and Kayla to the leader, "Marvin," who babbles on for a while about how South Redondo Beach High School used to be "back in the day." The band has two older gentlemen with long gray hair tuning their guitars. They seem to be staying up a little later than normal tonight as the much younger bandmates are doing most of the setup.

"Kayla, you need to get your outfit on; it's almost time. You girls both did such a great job," declares Mrs. Berz. "Organizing this dance is just like running your own business. From working with you two this past year, I can see you'll both be very successful someday. We need to see more girls like you in leadership roles. Thank you for all your help. Now, I need to go see how the traffic and parking situation is going. I will see you during the dance. Have fun!"

Both girls respond with a bubbly "thank you!"

Kayla and Sarah grab their backpacks and head to go change when Sarah feels someone tapping her leg. "Andrew! Look at you; did I know you were coming?"

Andrew has a wide smile and is standing proudly in a lobster costume with oversized gloves as claws, looking very orange.

"I found the costume the other day. I wanted to surprise you. It was hard keeping it a secret," explains Kathrine.

Sarah bends to one knee and touches Andrew's costume. "I like surprises, and this is a pretty good one," she exclaims as she hugs her little brother.

From the other side of the cafeteria, Shane sees Andrew and comes over. "Andrew, you look super cool, lobster boy," he says as they high five.

Andrew, standing proudly, asks his big brother, "Where's your shirt?"

Kathrine jumps in with "Good question, Andrew," as Harry and the other shirtless boys come over to them.

"We didn't want to get sweaty while we were working," remarks Shane.

Andrew sizes up the guys standing there and says to his mother, "Mom?...."

Kathrine answers before the question even comes out, "No, Andrew, you cannot take your shirt off like the other boys. Please keep your costume on. You look so cute."

Andrew, remembering how festive he looks in his lobster costume, quickly moves on.

"It's almost time. We have to go get 'the mermaid' ready. I haven't seen Coach Dan--is he here?" asks Sarah.

Kathrine playfully responds, "My date, Dan. Yes, he's outside keeping an eye on the crowd."

Kayla and Sarah both grab their stuff and head to their changing room as Shane and his friends find their shirts and put them on. "I'm out of here," says Shane as he gives his mom a hug goodbye.

"You guys too old to go to a dance?" asks Kathrine.

"We were never going; we were just here to help Sarah with the setup. We have some friends performing in *Mamma Mia!* at the Hermosa Theater; we're going there tonight," responds Shane.

Kathrine gets a text from Sarah asking her to come back to the dressing room to please help them. Shane tags along as he's waiting for Harry to get out of a conversation with his old girlfriend Dee, who's on the dance committee. Kathrine and Shane enter the room to find Kayla laying out on the table in a very sharp looking purple mermaid outfit. The form-fitting outfit includes a long, wide tail that starts above the waist. Kayla's midriff is bare, but she is wearing a bathing-suit top with plastic clams covering her chest. Sarah is standing behind Kayla, combing out her hair while clipping on a daisy flower.

Kathrine excitedly says, "Wow! You look beautiful."

Kayla responds exuberantly, "I'm really happy with all of it," and with a sly smirk "except, we just have one little problem..."

"Kayla can't walk because her feet are in the tail. we have to find some people to carry her out to the table. The doors are opening any minute; this was poor planning," interrupts Sarah.

Shane standing there amused listening to the conversation interjects, "I can go find the others, or…" Shane stops talking and turns his attention to a hand dolly that is standing against the wall with five cases of water stacked on it. He walks over to the dolly and takes the cases of water off and drops them on the floor. Shane wheels the hand dolly over to Kayla and laughingly says, "Get on, Kayla! Just stand on this. I'll tilt it back and walk the dolly with you on it over to the table."

"It's not perfect, but that will work. Shane, please don't drop her," pleads Kathrine.

With Shane holding the dolly upright, Kathrine and Sarah help Kayla to hop onto the bottom of the dolly, tucking in her tailfin so it's not dragging on the floor. The girls steady Kayla as Shane tilts the dolly back, and Kayla leans with it.

"Apparently mermaids aren't very heavy; she's actually pretty light," exclaims Shane.

"I guess you could call me a 'Little Mermaid!!' Get it!!" responds Kayla laughing while high-fiving with Sarah.

"You two are losing it and the dance hasn't even started yet," says Shane.

Sarah opens the door as Shane pushes and steers Kayla on the handheld dolly out into the dance. Shane, weaving his way through a few people while drawing some laughs, gets Kayla to her table without any issues.

Mrs. Berz, who sees everything, comes over to Kayla. "Now that's what I mean by getting creative," she says as Shane's buddies, who watched Shane wheel Kayla out, come over to help lift her onto the table.

Sarah combs Kayla's hair again as Kathrine organizes the shells, starfish, and other ocean ornaments that go around Kayla on the table. Shane and some committee members start taking selfies with "Kayla the Mermaid" as their background.

Mrs. Berz checks the clock on the wall and walks over to the band area and pulls out the microphone. "We are about to open the doors. I want to thank everyone from the food, decorations, ticket sales, setup, security, fundraising, and music committees who helped put this incredible event together; you all deserve a big round of applause." Everyone claps with enthusiasm and big smiles on their faces. Mrs. Berz announces loudly into the microphone, "The Enchantment Under the Sea dance is under way. Please open the doors!"

Joey Smoak, Lou, and Jaime are outside watching the crowd file through the doors into the dance and observing the ticket-sales operation. A few groups of people are just hanging outside deciding if it's worth the fifteen bucks to attend. Joey and his boys have been drinking in the woods behind the high school since they got here.

Lou a little sloppy, slurs, "There's a ton of cute girls here. Who knew this dance would be so good."

"Focus, you idiot," Joey complains as he gives Lou a look of disgust. "That's the second time I've seen that vice principal lady take money out of those metal boxes, put it into some shopping bag, and bring it inside."

The three boys walk up closer to the school windows and take a look inside to observe the activities.

"Vice Principal Ardito's office is right down that hallway from the cafeteria. She must be bringing the money back to her own office," guesses Joey.

"Do you know if the key you have works on her office door?" questions Jaime.

"The key definitely works on her office. I've been in there once before," says Joey proudly.

Jaime and Lou both jump in the air and chest bump each other like they just made the winning shot in the state basketball championship.

"Stop drawing attention to us." Joey glares at them. "You need to get your act together. I hope this wasn't a mistake bringing you two morons."

"We chill, we chill. Just a little buzzed. We got this," mumbles Lou.

Joey, taking a long look around the high school, sees the parked police car and pauses for just a moment but continues with his plan. "Good, let's get inside," he whispers.

Shane and his buddies get their goodbyes in as they head out of the dance. While walking to the car their attention is drawn to a bunch of empty beer bottles thrown on the grass. As they drive out of the parking lot, Shane glances to his left to see three guys about to turn the corner to go behind the high school; one of them looks like Joey Smoak.

Chapter 15
CHEESE AND FRUIT PUNCH

THE SOUNDS OF Marvin Berry and the Starlighters are ringing through the dance as the band plays the late fifties classic "La Bamba." There are a few brave students out there dancing, while others are still finding the nerve to take the plunge. Sarah is standing next to the table with "Kayla the Mermaid" and greeting people as they enter through the whale arch. The dance looks festive, and people have been complimenting them on how great the decorations look.

"It's so crowded. I love it," exclaims Sarah.

Both girls are enjoying all the attention they're receiving. Sarah calls over Evan from the food table, interrupting the creation of his cheddar cheese castle on his plate. "Evan, congrats again. You played so great this weekend. Thanks for all your help catching for me," says Sarah.

Evan, not used to getting compliments from girls looks down at the floor acting all shy, replies "Thank you."

Some of the softball girls, Annemarie, CeCe, Katt, and Mia, enter the dance and come over to Sarah. The girls are all excited to be here and hug each other as if they haven't seen each other in a hundred years.

Sarah feeling like a hostess articulates, "Evan, do you know Annemarie?"

Evan confidently steps over to both of them and reaches out his hand to shake Annemarie's. "I do now," he declares.

Annemarie's face lights up a little surprised by Evan's confident style.

"My favorite catchers," Sarah says as she puts her arms around each of them and smiles to take a selfie with Annemarie's phone.

Evan and Annemarie, already engulfed in some conversation about why Swiss cheese has holes, head over to the food table together.

Sarah, noticing how quickly Evan and Annemarie seem to have gotten along, thinks, *I guess anything's possible.* Her thoughts wander to how Stryker's night is going. Sarah is tempted to check her phone, but she and Kayla made a deal to stay in the moment; no phones.

Joey leads Jaime and Lou to the back of the school where Joey unlocks a door to the school's auditorium with his master key. The boys go in cautiously, not knowing if security or anybody else is around. They head down a hallway to an inside delivery door that is attached to the cafeteria; Joey opens this door with his key as well. They walk down the short hallway and into the dance.

Lou stammers, "That was easy. Let's get this party started," as he starts dancing in place to "Beat It" by Michael Jackson and checking out the girls walking by as he discreetly takes a swig of his half-empty flask of whiskey.

"This place is tripping, dude! They have a food table. I need some grub. I'm starving," says Jaime.

Joey, angry and slurring his words, grumbles, "You guys are a horror show. Are we going after the money or not?"

Lou takes charge. "I know where Ardito's office is. Let me go check it out and see if anyone is around," he scowls as Joey grabs the whiskey flask from him and takes a drink. Lou grabs it back and stuffs it in his jacket.

"Great, go see what you can find. If you run into anyone, just tell them you're looking for the bathroom," mutters Joey.

Lou slowly heads to the hallway while burping loudly in front of a group of girls sitting at a table who seem grossed out by his antics.

Joey puffs out his chest and declares, "Trouble, here we come."

Sarah, relaxed and animated, is busy chatting with other committee members about how great the dance is going. She's still standing next to "Kayla the Mermaid" as the line going past Kayla into the dance has been gone for a little while now.

"I love being the mermaid, but another fifteen minutes on the table and I'll be ready to change out of this and dance," Kayla comments eagerly.

The dance floor is very full now as many of the kids have gotten over their early dance jitters. The disco ball that Mrs. Berz loves is spinning and flickering light onto the dance floor as the bodies keep moving up and down. The band has their own oscillating lighting, which is just adding to the dance-floor vibe. The music is loud, and this is definitely a party.

Evan comes walking over to Sarah with some urgency in his step as Annemarie follows. "I don't know if you know this, but Joey Smoak is here."

All the gleam and excitement from the dance instantly leaves Sarah's face as she looks around the dance floor, searching for Joey.

"Did he just say what I think he said? Smoak is here?" asks a concerned Kayla.

Sarah is feeling a little numb from the news. "Apparently, but I haven't seen that loser yet."

Annemarie grabs Evan's hand as she pulls him out on the dance floor. Sarah stands with Kayla at the table as CeCe, Mia, and Katt remain next to them in a small circle, dancing in place, while CeCe makes silly fruit-punch moustaches with her drink.

"What are you going to do?" Kayla asks.

Sarah, coming out of her momentary shock, responds, "I'm going to do nothing. We came here to have a good time tonight and that is what we are going to do. Joey's not ruining this night."

Sarah's best laid plans do not work out, as Joey, from across the dance floor, sees Sarah and Kayla and walks directly over to them. Sarah, standing at the table, stiffens up, not knowing what to expect.

Joey, sounding like a happy drunk, mumbles to Kayla, "Well hello little mermaid. Where have you been all my life?" Joey's now standing directly next to Sarah but ignoring her. He hops onto the Mermaid table to get closer to Kayla so he can speak more clearly to her.

Kayla, who has only heard about Joey does not seem very comfortable with Joey's sloppy flirting, answers quietly to his question, "In the ocean?"

Joey leans into Kayla a little closer and starts feeling her legs through her purple costume. "This is some nice material you've got here. These your fins?"

Kayla with the look of fear in her eyes tries turning away from Joey.

Sarah steps in. "Smoak, why don't you just get the hell off the table. You smell like booze and are obviously drunk. You're a mess."

Joey bellows loudly, "Why don't you mind your own business, bitch." He then gets louder and slurs his words. "Oh, the *big* hero, the *big* softball star, the *big* baseball player. Somebody else is getting the attention, and you can't handle it. Sounds like you're the mess!"

The softball girls and other students near the mermaid table turn their focus to how loud and animated Joey is acting. Joey continues angrily, no longer sounding like a happy drunk.

"You're lucky that guy was there to step in front of me during that softball crap because I was going to beat your ass."

Sarah, taken aback by Joey's aggressiveness, takes a step away from the table.

Jaime reappears. He leans into Joey while placing his hand on his shoulder and whispers, "Lou says the money is there. The office is empty. Bring the key. Let's do this now."

Joey listens to Jaime for a few seconds and adamantly announces, "When I'm done here."

Jaime steps back, surprised by Joey's response, and leans in again to Joey, trying to make his point. "The money is there! It's clear now!" Jaime repeats.

Joey ignores Jaime and just sits back down on the table, turning all of his attention back to Kayla. "Now, where were we before we got interrupted?" Joey resumes rubbing Kayla's tailfins.

"Take your hands off my leg," implores Kayla, feeling more and more uncomfortable.

Joey continues his creepy advances. Kayla wants to get up and just run away but can't because of her costume. Joey slides even closer to Kayla on the table and starts rubbing her bare arms with his hand.

Kayla aggressively says, "Please stop touching me."

Joey ignores Kayla's plea as Sarah can now see Kayla tearing up.

Sarah steps closer to Joey and states with anger, "Take your damn hands off of her!"

Joey immediately stops and stands up, toe to toe with Sarah, looking directly in her eyes. In a cocky and taunting manner asks, "And what are you going to do about it? Joey waits a few seconds, "Nothing, just like I thought."

Sarah pauses for a quick second, thinking how her mom might handle this and, in an instant, pulls her right arm back, and quickly and decisively with all her pent-up Joey Smoak frustration and strength, punches Joey Smoak square in the face.

Joey, clearly not expecting to be drilled by a girl, falls back hard onto the punch table as it collapses. The punch bowl goes flying into the air with cups, napkins, pretzels, and assorted cheeses. Joey, laying on his back on top of the collapsed table, has a look of astonishment on his face as blood drips from his nose and Jaime leans over to try to help him up. Joey, still dazed, struggles to get up alone as Jaime now takes an aggressive step to come at Sarah.

CeCe and Katt, who have watched the whole altercation, take a combative step in front of Sarah to block Jaime's path.

CeCe says in her father's loud military tone, "Stand down, son," as she stands rigid, waiting to attack.

Jaime, who clearly did not anticipate girls standing up to him, reconsiders his actions as he pauses and turns back to help Joey.

Coach Dan and the security guards quickly arrive to grab Joey and Jaime and lead them by their arms out of the dance. As things calm down for a second, Sarah's friends come running over. Mia and Annemarie arrive together.

"Are you OK? I can't believe you punched Joey Smoak," says Annemarie looking impressed.

Sarah turns to CeCe and Katt saying, "Thanks for stepping up; I don't know what that lunatic would have done."

CeCe, still feeling her adrenaline rush, hugs Sarah. "Softball girls got your back. Oh man, that was so crazy. I bet that dude is glad he backed down because I would have kicked his ass," she says as all the girls start high-fiving and laughing.

Nearby, a group of students are posting video and pictures of the incident on social media.

Kathrine comes running over to Sarah. "What the hell just happened? Are you hurt?"

"Joey was so drunk he kept putting his hands all over Kayla," Sarah says. She asked him to stop a bunch of times, but he ignored her. Then he got in my face, so I just smacked him in his, and for the record, my hand is killing me. Could someone find me some ice."

Katt jumps into action and heads to the back of the kitchen looking for the ice machine.

"Coach Dan and security came over and took Joey away. He's a freaking nightmare," says Sarah.

The euphoria of the moment ends quickly as Vice Principal Ardito arrives. Hearing the music blaring and all the commotion still in the air, Mrs. Ardito suggests, "We should all go find a quiet place to talk."

Sarah helps Kayla take off her mermaid outfit discreetly before Vice Principal Ardito leads a group including Kayla, Sarah, and her mom out of the cafeteria and into an adjacent hallway where she finds an empty classroom. Inside, the chairs are in a semicircle and a half-finished crossword puzzle is on the board. Coach Dan arrives as they enter the classroom. Sarah and Kayla take a seat while the adults continue standing.

Kathrine, now knowing that her daughter is OK from her little skirmish, moves into mother mode. "You can't be punching people, Sarah. What if you really hurt that boy? You can be suspended, maybe even arrested! This is still a school!"

Kayla, sitting there listening, jumps in and tries to explain. "Joey was so drunk, he just kept coming over and putting his hands on me saying, 'Let's slow dance, baby.' They weren't even playing a slow song! Sarah and I both told him to stop, but he just kept touching me. He was slurring his words and getting more aggressive."

Vice Principal Ardito listens intently as Coach Dan joins the conversation. "Kayla, did you feel threatened? Did Joey assault you?"

"Yes, definitely! He was hurting my arms when he was grabbing at me. I didn't want him rubbing my legs. I told him to stop and he wouldn't. I was scared. I couldn't just walk away because of my mermaid tail," Kayla further explains.

Coach Dan, standing directly next to Kayla with a comforting hand on her shoulder, advises, "We should call your parents and let them know what happened here tonight to see if they want to file charges, which I think you should."

Coach Dan and the Vice Principal take a step out of the classroom and have a private conversation then Dan leaves the building and goes outside to see if the police are still with Joey.

Vice Principal Ardito steps back into the classroom and calmly says, "Sarah, what you did sticking up for your friend is a very noble thing to do. But you could have gotten security, your mom, or any one of the dance chaperones and told us about Joey. She slowly paces the room but looks directly at Sarah and continues, "We can't have people punching other people at school."

"I'm sorry, but I knew Kayla was in trouble," says Sarah.

Mrs. Ardito pauses for a few moments and runs her hand through her hair and lets out a deep sigh. "This is what I'm going to do. I will take the rest of the weekend to think about some punishment for you, and please understand this is very serious. You can come see me first thing Monday morning in my office to discuss your punishment."

Sarah, really starting to feel like she's in some kind of serious trouble, mutters, "Thank you."

"But in the interim, let's get some ice on that hand. I'll go talk to the police, and if my watch is correct, you still have thirty minutes left in the dance," observes Mrs. Ardito. "Kayla, I'll make an appointment for you to speak with one of the school counselors first thing on Monday," she gently says as Kayla nods her head yes.

Vice Principal Ardito turns to leave the room while smiling at Kathrine, who also responds with a "thank you," and a cautious smile on her face.

Sarah and Kayla both get up from the chairs and immediately start hugging.

"I love you!" says Kayla.

"I love you too," says Sarah.

"This has been one wild dance," continues Kayla.

"I know, and it's not even over yet."

Kathrine comes over to hug both of them. Kayla heads out of the classroom first. Kathrine stops Sarah. "Please know I'm very proud of you for sticking up for Kayla."

"I know you are, Mom. Joey was getting really scary. I had to do something. I did just what you would have done."

* * *

Stryker is having trouble adjusting his eyes to the bright lights of intermission. The first half of the play was entertaining enough for a local performance and the music was very festive. Stryker listens to Madison and her parents discuss the play, as his mind wanders to Sarah and the dance.

He looks at his phone and has received no response to the texts he had sent her earlier. *I'm sure she's busy having fun.*

"I'm going to the restroom. Does anyone need anything?" Stryker pleasantly asks.

"I think we're all good," answers his dad, as the others smile and give courtesy waves.

Stryker is frustrated as he realizes the long winding line he's approaching is the one for the men's bathroom. He takes out his phone to pass the time while waiting when he is surprised to see a text from Evan.

"What the hell......."

* * *

Kathrine is reassured by Sarah and Kayla that they are fine and want to go back into the dance for the last thirty minutes. They head back inside as Coach Dan returns to the building, giving the thumbs up to the group as he stops to update the Vice Principal.

With the music still blaring and the dance in full swing, Katt hands Sarah a bag of ice. "Sorry it took so long, I had to go to the training room. Fortunately, the invitational track meet ran late, and there were some girls still getting treatment. I have sticky tape to secure it around your hand."

"Thank you so much," says Sarah as Katt wraps the tape around the ice so it stays secure on her hand without requiring her to hold it. Sarah enjoys her few moments of celebrity status as students and friends come by to relive her punch and take pictures.

Coach Dan comes over with Mrs. Berz and pulls Sarah to the side for a moment. "I want you to know that when Shane was leaving the dance, he got my number from your mom and texted me that Joey was outside with some other guys."

"He did?" Sarah responds surprised.

"Yes, with all that went on at baseball today, we kept an eye on the three of them. At some point one of the guards found this kid Lou drunk, snooping around the offices in the hallways. We took him inside to one of the classrooms and put the fear of God into him. Apparently, he's a God-fearing boy. Once I found the knife on him, I threatened him with felony charges, which was really me just stretching the truth. He quickly got very honest and told us about Joey's plan with this other kid Jaime to rob the money from the dance. I guess Joey had a master key, and they were going to use it to get into Vice Principal Ardito's office."

Sarah again stands there a little stunned.

Coach Dan continues, "They never had a chance to rob the dance and their whole plan fell apart once you punched Joey."

Sarah, flabbergasted by Coach Dan's comments, looks at Mrs. Berz, who gives Sarah a smile and a hug and states, "You did very good tonight, young lady."

Sarah's emotions are still swirling. "Coach Dan, thanks for everything. I'm really glad you're here tonight, and I'm really glad you and my mom are dating. I'm sorry I haven't said that to you sooner," says Sarah.

"That is very nice of you to say, Sarah. I'm very happy to be dating your mom as well. I'm just glad you're OK, *Rocky*," he says while playfully shadow boxing with her.

Sarah grabs a seat with the softball girls and takes a few minutes to try and relax and collect her thoughts. The dance floor is full and bouncing; being led by Evan and Annemarie. The light show is in full effect as there is a new electricity in the air. Marvin Berry and the Starlighters are as good as advertised and cranking out the tunes. The movie *Back to the Future*, projected on the wall, has reached the dance scene where they are taking Biff away. There are tables of kids watching the movie and laughing at the evening's similarities.

Sarah gets a good laugh as she looks up to see Andrew, whose costume is long gone, sliding across the stage shirtless with lots of encouragement from Marvin and the Starlighters. The band is cranking out "Johnny B. Goode" as Kathrine tries grabbing Andrew from the stage as he runs behind the drummer for cover. Andrew is clearly not done with the dance.

Sarah, adjusting the tape holding her ice pack to her hand, looks up to see someone approaching her from the entrance. With all the lights swirling in the darkness and the size of the crowd it takes a moment for Sarah to determine who it is.

"Stryker, what are you doing here?" asks Sarah.

Stryker sits down next to Sarah. "We were out at the show and I looked at my phone during intermission. There were over fifty posts about you punching out Joey Smoak at the dance. Social media has tons of pictures of Joey laying out on a broken table. At first, I thought it was blood all over his shirt, until I saw the empty punch bowl, then realized it's probably just Hawaiian punch."

"It was probably a little of each," says Sarah.

"I want to say I'm sorry I wasn't here. With all the insanity from the game today and this being your event, I really should have been here with you tonight," says Stryker.

"That's nice of you to say. I would have liked to see you too," Sarah replies honestly as they both look into each other's eyes with genuine smiles. "I know you had people visiting," continues Sarah.

"About that...our family friends who are visiting, I didn't mention that one of the girls, Madison, was my girlfriend for a while. We had worked the dances together in Fresno. Part of the reason I stopped coming to the Enchantment meetings was it felt awkward for me to do the same things with you that I had done with my ex."

"You were thinking like that about me?" asks Sarah.

"Yes, we broke up when I moved down here, so the whole thing was a little uncomfortable. But we talked about it earlier and we've both moved on. I was thinking about you all night. I tried texting you but heard nothing. Then when I saw everything about you punching Joey, I just had to come. I left the play and told my mom it was an emergency."

Sarah pauses, smiling brightly and says, "I'm really glad you're here."

"Me too. I didn't even mind having to pay for the last fifteen minutes of the dance," states Stryker.

Sarah is startled as Shane comes up from behind her and gives her a huge bear hug. "What are you doing here? I thought you left," says a surprised Sarah.

"Well, we were watching the play and at intermission I saw Stryker there with his family. He told me what happened with you and Joey, so I thought I would come back to check up on you."

"I'm doing fine now though my hand's a little sore. Coach Dan told me you texted him about Joey being here, thank you!"

"Just watching out for my sis; that comes with being the man of the house," says Shane smiling.

"Well I'm glad you're the man of our house too," adds Sarah proudly.

Shane continues chatting while smiling, "and I was wrong about one thing."

"And what was that?" responds Sarah.

I guess you are kind of like Mulan."

"Very funny Shane. All I know is Mulan must have needed a lot of ice," says Sarah smiling while adjusting her wrapped hand.

Marvin Berry is making some announcements: "This event is about keeping our ocean clean. Please go to the 'Motion in the Ocean' website to find out ways you can help accomplish that or just by making a donation." Marvin gives out the website for Friends of the Library, promoting the great South Redondo Beach library system. "Get educated, use the resources, we need everyone's help to keep the oceans clean and safe." The mood of the dance is fun and festive as the night is winding down. Marvin Berry finishes up with "As we do every year, just like in the Enchantment Under the Sea dance in *Back to the Future*, our last song of the night will be a slow romantic one, *Earth Angel*."

Some of the casual dancer's scurry off the floor, as many couples slowly start making their way onto the dance floor including Evan and Annemarie for the final dance.

Stryker, sitting with Sarah, leans in and asks, "Would you like to have our first dance?"

Sarah smiles back at Stryker and stands up from the table. "Yes, I would, as long as you don't mind getting your shirt a little wet."

Shane, who is looking at his phone, feels a gentle tap on his shoulder. It's Kayla.

"It's been a wild night, and I haven't danced once. Would you like to dance?" she asks.

"Sure, why not" as he quickly stuffs his phone in his pocket. "This is your party. Plus, I've never danced with a mermaid before," declares Shane smiling.

"And I've never danced with a surfer," replies Kayla.

"Perfect, we're like two fish out of water," remarks Shane as he leads Kayla to the dance floor.

Sarah and Stryker walk onto the dance floor hand in hand as the droplets of water slowly drip onto the dance floor from her melting ice pack. The dance floor fills up to the sounds of the song "Earth Angel." Sarah sees her mom and Dan on the dance floor as well. She purposely dances away from them and closer to the band. Andrew, now with his shirt back on, is sitting at an empty table playing games on his mom's phone. Stryker takes Sarah's hand and holds it close to his chest as Sarah puts her other hand on his shoulder.

"I'm sorry if I'm getting your shirt wet, but my hand is still pretty sore."

Stryker, happy to be there with Sarah, responds, "I'm fine."

Sarah laughs to herself thinking *Yes you are!*

Stryker continues, "I have plenty of other shirts."

Sarah leans in a little closer as they both sway back and forth to the beat of the music. "This may have been the craziest day of my life. But I could not have asked for a more perfect ending," says Sarah.

Stryker and Sarah lock eyes on each other and hold each other's gaze for a few seconds as Sarah leans in to give Stryker a short kiss.

Stryker says, "That was nice," as they continue to dance slowly. Stryker then leans in to give Sarah a long and extended kiss as they both embrace. *Who doesn't love the Enchantment Under the Sea dance!*

Marvin Berry and the Starlighters make an announcement thanking everyone for coming as the song and the dance slowly come to a close. Many couples are still lingering on the dance floor hoping to continue their night. Stryker and Sarah are one of those couples who look like they would rather be nowhere else as they continue hugging and kissing. Sarah and Stryker both release from their comfortable embrace as Coach Dan and Kathrine approach them. Sarah doesn't know if her mom had been watching her kissing Stryker.

Kathrine gives Sarah a big hug. "We're heading home. Andrew is ready for bed. Let me know if you need a ride home after cleanup. I'll have Shane come and get you."

Sarah thanks her mom and Coach Dan, gives sleepy Andrew a hug, and turns her attention back to Stryker. As Dan and Kathrine begin walking away, Sarah turns to her mom and cutely asks, "Mom, how was your date night working with Dan?"

Kathrine stops walking, holding Andrew in one arm with his head on her shoulder, looking directly back at Sarah with a big smile on her face. "Apparently, not as good as yours," as Dan and Kathrine both fist bump each other, smiling brightly as they head to the exit.

"Finally, Mom, you've said something funny!" replies Sarah laughing.

Chapter 16
GRATEFUL

■■
■■

SARAH IS COMMENTING to her mom that the winding-road entrance into the cemetery seemed a much longer drive today than on the day of Grandpa's funeral. This is their first-time visiting Grandpa Al's grave since he passed away a month ago. They drive around a long twisting line of cars with their lights on that are waiting for a funeral procession to begin. Sarah remembers waiting in that line. She keeps nervously looking at her phone even though it shows no new messages. Kathrine is trying to understand the map they were given at the guard shack when they entered, looking for Grandpa Al's location, which the attendant had highlighted in red.

"I'm pretty sure this is the section. All of these trees do look familiar, and here's the pond with the ducks," says Kathrine as they pull into the mostly empty parking lot. As they make their way across the grass, they see a wooden directional sign posted that points them to Grandpa Al's area.

Sarah was a little surprised when her mom suggested going to see Grandpa Al at the cemetery. Shane declined his invitation. He said he wasn't ready to emotionally deal with going to the cemetery yet. Plus, the surf was pretty good today.

Kathrine felt it was easier having Andrew on a play date with a friend on their first visit. She was glad it was just the two of them This was the first time Sarah has had to deal with a death in her life and it has not been easy. Kathrine explains to Sarah what they'll do when they get to the grave site. Those plans bring a smile to Sarah's face and helps her relax a little.

Sarah counts off aloud, "Section C, Row 7. Section C, Row 8. Two more. Section C, Row 10; here it is."

They stand before the newly installed gray granite headstone reading the engraved words:

Albert Richardson, In Loving Memory

Kathrine puts her arm around Sarah and holds her close. "It's hard seeing his name there," Kathrine says as she tears up and sniffles, "but I know he's in a better place, and all the pain is gone."

Kathrine and Sarah take a few minutes to compose themselves as Sarah grabs the beach blanket they brought and lays it down on the grass. They sit quietly for a while. Kathrine places the yellow daisies they brought next to the headstone and pulls a sandwich out from her bag and happily splits it with Sarah. Kathrine shares the story about Grandpa Al making his own funeral arrangements. He wanted it simple and not a financial burden on the family. They sit peacefully for what seems like hours. Kathrine suggests they start heading out as Sarah has a home softball game today.

Sarah brushes a few leaves and some dirt off the headstone as she begins talking. "We all miss you, Grandpa; it's been hard without you," she says as a few tears drip from her eyes, "but I know you would be proud of me for pitching; my knuckleball was darting and moving just like you showed me. I love you."

Kathrine stands next to Sarah, gently rubbing her back. "We can stop by again soon," she adds as the two of them pick up their stuff and start walking back to the car.

Sarah suddenly stops and says, "I almost forgot—the ball!"

Kathrine reaches into her backpack and pulls out the game ball Sarah was awarded for pitching in her first baseball game in the Enchantment tournament and hands it to her.

Sarah turns back to the headstone and gently places the baseball on the ground next to the yellow daisies. "I want you to have my game ball; none of it was possible without you." Sarah slowly leans over and gently kisses her grandfather's headstone and quietly turns to walk with her mom.

"Your grandfather would be so proud of you for how you've handled everything, honey, as am I."

"Thank you. I know the way he helped our family and handled his cancer; I'm really proud of him too," pronounces Sarah.

* * *

The softball game versus Del Amo High School is about to begin, but this day is already a success. While warming up before the game, Sarah sees the little softball player Kelli and her mom, who had come to watch the game. Sarah jogs over to both of them and gives them a big hug and explains to them that, yes, that *was* Sarah dressed like a boy for the baseball tryout. Sarah describes her class project and how she felt so badly that she could not say anything to Kelli at the time. Sarah takes out some wristbands and a batting glove and gives them to Kelli to thank her for being such a great fan.

Kelli happily responds, "I knew that was you Sarah! I knew it."

Sarah is very happy to be back playing softball full-time. She recalls being pleasantly surprised and amused when she saw the Monday headline for the school newspaper last week, which read "Baseball Tournament Win Packs A Punch." Kathrine enjoyed the clever headline as well when she read it but was hoping to keep her daughter's "adventure" a little quieter.

Sarah sits in the dugout and grabs her bag looking for a hair band. She comes across the suspension letter she had stuffed in her bag from that Monday morning meeting with Vice Principal Ardito for punching Joey, where she learned about being suspended for the day. Sarah was also required to take an online anger-management assessment. Her mom had gotten over her initial frustration of Sarah punching Joey and was mellow about it all now.

After that Monday morning meeting, Sarah happily went home and went back to bed until one o'clock. She remembers that Stryker's school day had ended early, and he was nice enough to stop by her house to bring her some lunch, but he was a little disappointed to find Kathrine had come home early as well. Best laid plans.

Later that same afternoon, Sarah finally had time for a nice discussion with Shane about him wanting to attend *Boston University* for college. Sarah also had a good chuckle when Shane told her he had asked Kayla to go bike riding. *I wonder if he'll be wearing his cologne?* she thought.

Coach Dan arrives at the game to find his last row seat saved by Kathrine and Andrew in the crowded home grandstand. All the attention Sarah had gotten through baseball generated plenty of interest in South Redondo Beach High School softball as well. Dan had just come from the police station and had further updates for Kathrine about Joey. "I know you're aware of some of the details. Mick Martin, Joey's foster parent had been called by the police to pick him up from the dance. Mick had told them he had been struggling with Joey and wasn't sure what he should be doing to help him. Mick has now taken Joey by Kayla's house and met with her and her parents as Joey apologized for his behavior."

"Kayla texted Sarah that Joey had come by her house too," says Kathrine.

Dan continues, "The police took back the stolen key from Joey. The other boys also had their parents called and received citations for drinking. Nothing ever came of the attempted robbery of the dance because the boys never got around to breaking into the office or stole anything. Those kids were lucky they didn't end up in jail."

"Do you think Sarah will hear from Joey?" asks a concerned Kathrine.

Dan, amused, says, "I didn't get the sense that would be happening. Joey must be a little embarrassed by being punched out like that. I'm sure he's seen the video of him laid out on the broken table numerous times. For all you know, Joey may be thinking he deserves an apology."

Kathrine laughs loudly at the last remark as Andrew, whose attention is drawn to two golden retrievers behind the backstop, starts climbing over her to get out of the stands. "Joey's been hit in the head by too many pitches if he thinks he'll get an apology from Sarah," quips Kathrine.

"Mick Martin talked about getting Joey some steady counseling, which is good to hear. He moved back into their house. I'm glad to see they're not giving up on him, and Joey is still trying," says Dan.

Andrew jumps from the last step of the bleachers and runs by a large group of guys walking toward the stands. Kathrine, seeing Andrew receive a few high fives along the way, realizes that the large group of boys is the South Redondo Beach baseball team. Kathrine turns to Dan and says, "You didn't tell me the boys were coming."

"I know nothing about it. The team put this together on their own."

The baseball boys come to the corner of the bleachers, waving to people they know. Kathrine sees that Dylan, still in his wheelchair, is with them as she climbs down to greet them. "This is a very nice surprise," Kathrine says to all of them.

Evan chimes in, "We just came from the hospital. Ryan and Teddy are getting released tomorrow and Jack in a few days. This was some great news we wanted to share."

"I'm so glad to hear the boys are going home soon," says Kathrine.

"We also wanted to come and support Sarah for all the help she gave us," says Dylan, as he wheels his chair into the shade while smiling brightly. "Plus, Stryker and Evan both have *girlfriends* on the team now."

Sarah finishes her warm-up tosses and heads over to the bench with Annemarie. She gives a wave to the baseball guys and smiles at Stryker. CeCe and Katt, who just noticed Dylan, both run over to quickly greet him.

Sarah sits on the bench, throwing a ball into her glove, as she waits for the umpire to start the game. *What an interesting little adventure it has been the last month. Grandpa passing, Mom and Coach Dan dating, trying out for baseball dressed like a dude, the accident, pitching in the baseball tournament, the dance, the punch, Stryker. But after all that's gone on, I'm right where I want to be. Happy and playing softball with the girls.*

The umpire calls the teams onto the field as the sound system plays upbeat party music while Sarah takes her final warm-up pitches. Annemarie comes out from behind the plate to offer some last-minute encouragement to Sarah while adding, "I've never played a softball game in front of my boyfriend before."

Sarah laughs and reassures her that everything will be fine while adding, "I guess I never have either."

The umpire yells, "Play ball." Sarah winds up and throws her first pitch. "Strike!" As she goes to the rubber for her second pitch, Sarah gets distracted by some commotion near the bleachers. She turns to see a little boy running as hard as he can, arms flying, as he crosses the third-base line heading toward second base. Katt, who is playing shortstop and smiling, doesn't even try to stop him.

The parents in the bleachers, all amused, turn their heads to Kathrine as she stands up and gives a loud and very animated yell. *"ANDREW!!!!!!"*

Cast of Characters

Andrew – youngest member of Trout family.
Annemarie – catcher on softball team, friend of Sarah.
Baseball Boys – Teddy, Sean, Jack, Ryan, Trevor
Coach Dan Sugimoto – high school baseball coach, T-ball coach, friend of Kathrine.
Coach Nevs – high school softball coach.
Dylan – friend, baseball player, grew up with Sarah and Shane.
Evan – catcher on the baseball team, friend of Sarah.
Grandpa Al Richardson – Kathrine's dad, grandfather to Sarah, Shane, Andrew.
Joey Smoak – baseball player.
Kathrine Trout – teacher, mom of Shane, Sarah, Andrew.
Kayla – friend of Sarah, Enchantment committee member.
Krista Stern – friend of Kathrine and neighbor, local newscaster.
Lana Berz – family friend, teacher, in charge of Enchantment dance.
Mick Martin – softball coach, foster parent.
Mr. Fairfield – guidance counselor.
Ruben Acevedo – Strike Four umpire.
Sarah Trout – sister to Shane and Andrew, softball player, Enchantment committee member.
Shane Trout – brother to Sarah and Andrew, surfer.
Shane's Friends – Harry Matthew, Will, Nico.
Softball Girls – Katt, Mia, CeCe.
Stryker Estrada – new student, baseball player, friend of Sarah.
Vice Principal Ardito – high school administrator.

About the Author

AWARD WINNING CHRISTMAS STAUDLE is an author, comedian, athlete, and family man who intertwines both his affinity for humor, and love for family, into his work. Inspired by his life's adventures from the shores of Long Island to the beaches of Southern California.

Mr. Staudle writes entertaining and heartfelt stories about sport, family, relationships, and community.

https://ground-rule-trouble.com

Made in the USA
Middletown, DE
03 November 2020